Creature Feature (collection two)

For my loving wife Carmel

1

INDEX

14—night time hell time

ONE

Boar

1

The piglet stayed close to its mother, it was barely two months old and already the piglet towered over its mother, the mother boar looked like the baby. But the piglet was still raw, it needed its mother to train him, the water in the river tasted bad today, but the piglet was thirsty and its mother drank too. They went out hunting together in the early evening, the heat of the day carried on into the night, the piglet found it easy to hunt the small animals, its sheer size no match for them, and he found he could pick up speed fast.

Its confidence was growing, the piglet heard a sound, a rushing of air and then heard its mother cry out, and the squeal was loud. The piglet came out of a group of trees, and saw its mother laying dead on the ground, a spear protruding from her belly, blood dripped into the pool already formed on the ground. The two hunters were laughing as they approached the dead boar, the piglet was already the size of a pony, and in that moment, it learned all about pain and hurt, and anger.

Already the male piglet had large sharp tusks coming out of its mouth, and they were higher than the long snout. The piglet raced at the men, they saw it late and didn't have time to react, the first hunter caught the full force of the tusks as they went deep into his belly, blood sprayed over the dead body of the boar, and the trees nearby.

The second hunter fell to the ground in shock looking at the huge beast the young piglet rounded on him, and stamped on the hunter's head. The hunters head exploded like a water melon, blood and gore splattering the ground. The piglet nudged its mother and let out a squeal, the smell of human flesh soon made the piglet hungry, and it began to feast on the fresh meat.

The man looked at the ground in front of him, Martin Hedge was a scientist and his field was the wild boar or wild pig or even razorback as they called them in North America. He was in India in the small village of Latur, but he stayed away from the main town and worked sorely in the countryside and woods. Yes, the town even had wild pigs walking around not in the least bit bothered by humans.

But it was here he could find out more about them in their natural inhabit, Martin was twenty-five and single, well who wanted a man that was never at home anyway. He was a good-looking man with blonde hair and blue eyes, his mother always said that when he was ill his eyes would go a bright blue color.

His thoughts were broken as his eyes fell on some hoof prints, no way could they be real; he kneeled down and looked closely. There was no doubt that they were boar prints, but the boar would have to be the size of a cow to do prints like that.

Boars generally reached between thirty-five to seventy inches in length and twenty-two to forty-three inches in height, this thing was a monster. He took out the cast mould and poured the stuff into the prints, he would look more closely back at the hotel, when the cast was set, he carefully put it into a container, and then back in his rucksack, and he stood and took some photographs. He shivered as he looked around the field and the trees of the forest close by, the mountains rose into the air, he had one last look around, and then headed back to the hotel close by.

2

In Latur you have the main town and on the out skirts you have lots of tiny villages called tribes, they even have a section in the local paper called tribal corner. The villagers in this one particular village were celebrating the feast of the beast for the next couple of weeks; the beast roamed the woods and ate men and women at its leisure. They celebration was to honor the beast, and make it leave them alone for another year.

The women dressed in loose saris, their breasts bobbing up and down as they danced round the open fire, the men sat and watched, eating rice and beans. The wooden huts stood around the tiny village like sentinels protecting them. The village was basic, wooden huts for sleeping mainly the cooking was done on an open fire outside, the twenty or so villagers lived as one family.

An old man stood up he needed to pee badly, he took one last look at the young girl with the erect nipples, and slowly made his way into the woods which surrounded them. The boar was hungry and could smell the smell of man, it had stood in the woods watching them dance around the fire, it had waited and then it had seen the man walking towards the woods. The boar had been sick all that day, its stomach would not hold anything down, but now in the evening it felt better and hungry.

The man let out a sigh as he let his line of urine go, he didn't hear the bushes moving to his left, he didn't see the head of the wild boar come out of the woods. The old man felt pain in his side, he put his hand there, and could feel the sticky wetness of his own blood, the boar came at him again this time thrusting with all its might, the tusks ripped the old man almost in half. The steaming intestines fell to the ground and the boar started to eat its meal, the boar raised its head, it could hear another voice coming towards the woods. The young female called her grand pa's name once again no reply; she made her way to the edge of the woods, and stood trying to see inside the darkness.

The giant boar came at her quickly, it was as big as a cow and was nearly as tall as the young girl, and it took her head in its mouth and crunched down. Blood sprayed out of the sides of its mouth as it crunched down on bone again and again. The villagers saw the beast at the edge of the woods and began running round like headless chickens, some of the men picked up sticks and lit them in the flames. They marched over to the woods to frighten the beast away, but the beast had already gone, all they found was the half eaten old man, and blood where the girl had stood.

Not too far from the tiny village lay the hotel, it was called a hotel, but in fact it looked like a cheap hippy hang out joint. Paint peeled from the walls and the glass windows looked as if they would fall out at any minute, but the place was cheap and the food was excellent.

Andy Carter lay on the bed in one of the rooms he shared with Dave Allen, Andy had long hair tied back in a pony tail he was a good-looking boy at twenty-one, and he was tall and lanky which the girls seemed to like. He like his friend Dave were in India to record a video for their friend and singer Brian hull, Dave was a year younger than Andy at twenty and unlike his friend he was short and fat, but he had the gift of the gab and was never short on girlfriends.

He sat drinking a glass of whisky, the room consisted of a bedroom with two singles in which the two were now in, a bathroom with a shower and a toilet you had to squat over to shit. It was a shit hole, but the food they served was excellent, and they all agreed on that one thing.

Brain Hull also lay on the double bed his girlfriend was standing looking out of the window, he had been singing since he could remember, he had been in various groups in his twenty-four years, but now was trying to make it big on his own. It had been his idea to come to India for a holiday and to record a music video for his song. Love me like crazy which had got some interest from record companies, now he wanted to back it up with a video.

Brain had a pleasant face, but this hid the fact that he hated being short, and had a huge chip on his shoulder about it. His girlfriend Julie Pitt looked out of the window; see could see fire far off, as if the villagers were having bonfires. Julie was a very petite girl with dark short hair, her face was pretty, but she had far too many spots, but this didn't distract from the fact she was a lovely looking girl.

The only other occupant in the small hotel was Martin Hedge the boar expert, he would be leaving soon and joining the professor in New Delhi to finish off the lecture tour with him. The professor had taught Martin everything he knew and he couldn't wait to get out of Latur and join him in the more modern city of New Delhi. Martin sipped from his glass of whisky, he could also see the fires far away in the distance, he thought about the hoof prints and shivered, what if that thing was out there now.

3

The next day early the villagers went on a hunt, the men carried spears and some had bows made out of wood and arrows tipped with the deadly poison from a breed of frog found in the forest nearby. They hunted for an hour, and when they came back to the village the men carried a large boar tied to a pole, the women rushed out to see the beast. It was a normal sized boar maybe a little larger, its belly was fat and full, the women got bushy making a new fire, and the village would eat well tonight.

Hunter stood back and watched the women getting the fire ready, he had come from this village, and they still accepted him as one of them even though he had left them five years ago. He made his money hunting and that was his name hunter and it wasn't always legal but who cared, he had heard of the deaths and looking at the dead boar he felt that would never have killed two grown people. He had also heard that a scientist was in town and was staying at the hotel close by, he needed to pay this man a visit, and he was worried for this former village.

Martin was having a shave when there came a knock on the door, he cursed as he cut himself, he looked in the small mirror it wasn't so bad. He walked over to the door and opened it, an Indian man stood there, he was handsome and had a big cheery smile on his face, but the eyes told another story, they were hard and cruel eyes. The man was as tall as Martin and held out his hand, "I'm hunter."

Martin took the hand and offered the man to come in; Hunter stepped over the threshold and into the small room.

"What can I do for you Hunter?"

"I heard a white scientist was in town, and that he was looking at boars."

Martin smiled at the handsome man, "News travels fast."

"Not really when we have five whites in a town that has rarely ever seen the white man."

"Oh yes you mean the others in this hotel I don't know them I think they are American."

"Yes, they are and you are English I take it."

"Yes, born and bred."

"I have a problem and want you help sir."

Martin had forgotten his manners, "Sorry please call me Martin."

The man nodded and went on, "My village just a mile from here was attacked last night."

Martin thought of the hoof prints in the dirt, "Attacked by what."

The man looked at Martin with his hard eyes, "A wild pig."

The villagers were at first scared of the white man, but soon as Hunter spoke to them, they came out and crowded round him. The head of the village looked Martin up and down and spoke to Hunter who stood besides Martin.

"He says they have killed the beast that attacked them last night."

Martin looked at the skinned dead boar which was slowly cooking over the fire.

"Tell him I found hoof prints yesterday, and that thing here is far too small."

Hunter spoke to the head man; the man shook his head no.

"He says the beast is dead and they don't need an outsider to help."

"Right let me have my say and translate all of it to him as I go okay."

Hunter nodded at him, "Good idea martin."

"The boar or wild pig or as the north Americans call it razorback grows to a height of twenty-two to forty-three inches roughly speaking and the length is between thirty-five and seventy-nine inches.

About the size of the one you have there," he pointed to the cooking boar.

"Now boars can reach up to seventy to a hundred and eighty kilos in weight the largest recorded case was two hundred kilos. Now boars will eat anything and I mean anything, if they came across a dead man then they would eat it."

He paused and looked at the dead boar, "The tracks I found yesterday suggest a boar the size of a cow, and if that's the case then it would have no fear at all of man."

He stopped and let Hunter finish the translation, Hunter sadly shook his head, and pulled Martin away from the village.

"It's useless the man says they have killed the beast, these are simple men Martin I just hope they will be safe tonight."

Martin nodded to him, "We done all we could," he shivered as he looked at the woods, and he had the feeling that something was watching him.

4

After the white man had gone the head of the village gave orders for the feast that night, again they would pray to the beast for forgiveness, and hope that the beast would spare them this time. The night was chilly after a scorching day's heat, the villagers sat round the camp fire eating the meat from the dead boar; soon it would be time to start the dancing. The young girl kept looking at the young man, he smiled at her the two were in love and soon they would tell the rest of the village, but for now they liked sneaking around the woods, and finding time to be together.

As soon as they announced they were seeing each other the marriage would follow fast as was the way of the village. The boy was the first to disappear into the woods, no one noticed as the other woman were getting ready to dance, the boy waited by a large tree.

The girl made as if to go into her hut then quickly ran round the back of the hut, no one had seen her, and she went into the woods and started to go round to where she had seen the boy disappear.

The boar was hurting badly, its head felt like it was going to burst open, but the hunger in its belly had to be satisfied. It went hunting again close to its lair, it would have left the village well alone but for the pain, it couldn't think straight.

For an animal of its size the giant boar padded quietly through the woods, it could sense someone nearby. Its head began to clear the pain going to a dull throbbing, the boar eyed the man standing by the tree, it was time to feed, and then it heard another sound. It looked to its left there was another human coming directly to the man by the tree, the boar changed direction, and headed for the girl.

The young man could see the outline of his woman as she made her way through the bushes and plants, something big came out from the side of her and it was fast, one minute he could see her shape the next she was gone without a sound. The man went to the spot, nothing no blood just the plants leaning over to one side as if something big had run through them. He heard a sound as he knelt down to look at the path, the huge shape came out of the forest and knocked into his body hard, the man's body flew into the air and hit a massive tree trunk head first.

The man's dead body fell to the ground the head at a funny angle, the neck broken from the force of the impact.

The men had been ordered not to pee in the woods alone after the night before; the villagers settled down, and began to watch the women dance around the fire. One man had a big problem and it had been this way since he was a kid, he couldn't pee if someone was close by, he had to be alone. The man got up and told the head of the village that he had to get something from his hut, he was allowed to go, and his hut was blocked by a hut in front, and could not be seen from the fire.

The man went round the back of his hut, all was quiet, and he drew the thin material away from his crutch, and took out his penis. He sighed as he let go of a long hot stream of piss, he had been holding it for ages. He looked up and let go of his penis, a huge face stared at him, it was a wild pig, but the thing was huge, he dropped his hands to his sides and stood there in shock. The massive head of the beast leaned forward and in one bite took off the man's penis; he looked down and screamed as blood pumped out of the gaping wound. He fell to his knees and the boar took off his head with one bite, the stump spurted blood into the night.

By the time the villagers got there it was over they saw the headless body of the man and the bushes swaying as if something had turned and ran back into them.

The boar dragged the two bodies back to its lair, he had been disturbed by the screaming man and the running villagers, he would take the bodies back and eat one now, and store the other for later. It moved inside its cave, the cave was narrow at the entrance about five-foot floor to ceiling, but then opened into a larger chamber, a round chamber about ten feet high by twelve. The boar pushed the body of the young girl over to one side and settled down on its rump, and began to rip at the young man's body.

5

Martin and Hunter moved through the bushes, the woods still looked very foreboding even in the day light, some parts of the forest the day light didn't even enter.

"Christ we are leaving ourselves open like this," Martin said sounding worried the boar could come at them from any angle.

"Don't worry my friend," Hunter tapped his rifle.

But he was a worried man that morning he had come to the village and discovered three more people dead, one body and two youngsters missing. He had gone to the hotel and told Martin, and he had agreed to help hunter. They had climbed a bit of the mountain earlier and were now high up, but the trees and under growth were still thick on the mountain sides making it difficult to see how high they had come.

"We have to look for some sort of cave, a creature that size would need a big cave."

Hunter nodded he agreed with that, but in all his years here he had never come across a large cave, but there were many miles of terrain he had not trodden. The two men started to chat about this and that and they both walked past the cave, it was slightly hidden by a large over hanging tree, but if they had looked, they would have spotted it.

The boar could hear the two men talking, they were very close, and they had woken it up from its sleep, it got ready to attack. It lay their rock solid its body tense ready to pounce, but the voices receded into the distance and the boars body relaxed once more. It would sleep till night time then go farther afield to hunt; the village would have to be left for a while until they got sloppy again.

The villagers were scared and the head of the village had all the men and women working, they had started digging the pits in the early morning heat. Now in the afternoon the pits were ready, men and women got busy sharpening wooden stakes, these stakes were then put at the bottom of the pits, over the pits they covered with large leafs. If the beast came back tonight, they would lure it into one of the stake pits.

The head of the village stood and looked on, his hands resting on his large round belly, he was pleased with the idea it was a pity they had not thought about it yesterday. Night fell over the village, and the men again seated around the fire watching the women dancing, they would mourn their dead soon enough but the celebrations had to go on, and the beast made happy.

6

God that damn security guard was getting on Brian's nerves, the simple bastard was walking round the building hitting a stick against the ground, and blowing a damn whistle. It was crazy if there were criminals about all they had to do was hide round the back till the guard came round making all his noise then leg it to the front and rob the place. Talk about silly, the security guards in the modern world would be quiet and sneak up on the thief's, here it seemed even the security were God damn cowards.

He looked away from the window and onto the bed, Julie was laying naked reading a novel, he felt his penis stiffen in his boxer shorts, time for a bit of loving. They had a good shoot today and he was in a good mood for a change, even a joke from Andy about small people had been laughed off, normally he would have smacked the cunt in the mouth, but not today. Half of the video was complete and it was going great. Brian moved over to the bed and Julie smiled at him when she saw his boxers and put down the novel. She held up her arms to him, the tiny mound of her soft black pubic hair looking so inviting to him.

Dave was asleep on the bed, the lazy fucker thought Andy as he drowned another whisky, it had been a good shoot today, but God he hated India, the insects the heat. These crappy rooms they rented, but it would soon be over another day of shooting then they would move on to the better New Delhi, and maybe get rooms a lot more comfortable than these.

The only one saving factor in this dump was the food, boy could that woman cook, he wasn't a great lover of curries but man they tasted like heaven and the poori bread was out of this world. The chair creaked as he leaned back and stretched, he reached out and picked up the half full whisky bottle, time for another peg he thought pouring the amber liquid into his empty glass.

Martin packed his small case, tomorrow he would be on his way to New Delhi to join the professor, he couldn't wait, and Latur was such a tiny backward place. The research had been good and finding the giant hoof prints had been amazing, but still he had not seen the beast if indeed there was a giant boar. Let's face it he thought, there was no sign of it, and it was big not easy to hide itself all of the time, unless its intelligence was better than they all thought.

The attacks on the villagers could have been some other animal and in their state of terror they mistaken it for a wild pig, there were bears and wolfs still left in India, even large group of monkeys could have done the damage. The more he thought about a giant boar the more he disbelieved it. He thought about the eighty's movie about the giant boar the size of a rhino Razorback now that had been a fun movie.

The old woman moved through the tall plants on the hotel grounds, Mansi had owned the hotel with her pig of a husband for twenty years before the old bastard had died of a heart attack. He had treated Mansi like a servant, she did all the work and he would lay around, and then put on a nice face for the guest. Well things hadn't changed much she still done all the work, but it least she didn't have that pig ordering her about. She was going to check on the washing, unlike the village women who bashed their clothes against dirty walls to clean them, Mansi owned a washing machine.

It was a luxury she could afford since the old bastard had left her a tidy sum of money. She heard the sound to her right, she couldn't see in the darkness, something must have climbed over the wall; a five-foot wall surrounded the property. She stood there maybe it was just some animal, in all her fifty years Mansi had never been scared of the dark, but now something was freezing the blood in her veins.

The boar was crazy, the headaches had now intensified and drove it mad, now the only thing on its mind was to kill as many humans as possible it had been them that had made the river taste bad. The old wall had been crumbling away for years, and a simple nudge from the huge boar had pushed the bricks into the garden, most falling on vegetation making hardly any noise.

The boar came at the old woman fast, its tusks went into her belly and the boar flicked its head up, the woman went flying into the air and landed with a thump on the dirt ground. The boar walked over and sniffed the lifeless body, maybe just a little food, its stomach rumbled, the headache raged on in its head. A little food would be good it thought, it took the humans arm and bit into the flesh, it tasted so good, but seconds later the boar vomited the food up. Now its rage was complete it couldn't take any more food and the headaches were growing worse, and it was the human's fault they would pain for its pain.

7

The security guard saw old Mansi going into the back garden, she would often go for walks in the evening it was no surprise to him. It was time for another check, he picked up his stick and put the whistle in his mouth, unbeknown to Brian in the upstairs room there was a reason for making so much noise in the countryside, the noise was to scare off wild animals. He rounded the building on the left side and stopped he could make out something big standing over by some trees, 'what the fuck was that' he thought.

He blew his whistle and tapped the stick against the side of the hotel, the thing moved at lightning speed. He held out his hands and the thing hit him hard, he managed to hold onto the tusks as the thing threw itself against the side of the hotel. Dust and a few of the roof slats fell down, the hotel rocked on its foundations. The security guard was badly hurt the impact had shattered his spine the thing paused against the building and them stepped back.

The man slid to the floor semi conscious, he saw the beast come at him, its hoofed feet stamping down on his head, and then blackness. The boar stamped down on the man, blood splattered around as the head squashed like a grape, the boar could sense more men inside, and it would spare no man this night.

Dave woke up, "What the fuck was that," he said as the hotel rocked and shook, Andy put his whisky glass down, "Fuck if I know," he said.

The two men looked at each other then at the door, "Let's go take a look okay," Andy said, Dave nodded, "Okay mate you first."

Brian lay down the hotel shook, Julie besides him moaned, "What was that," he brushed her hair away from her pretty face, "Don't worry Diny its nothing to worry about go back to sleep."

He had always called her Diny because she was so tiny, but tiny didn't sound nice was it had become Diny and that's how it stayed. He looked towards the window and thought, 'what the fuck had that been' he could hear his two friends in the hallway they would go and see.

Andy came out of the room first closely followed by Dave he looked up and down the empty corridor.

"Maybe we should knock Brain up," and Dave said looking at his friend's door, "Hell no let them be," Andy replied.

There came a crash from downstairs it sounded as if something had smashed through the front porch and door way, wood smashed against the walls and ground as something big came into the hotel lobby.

Martin looked out the window in horror; he had heard and felt the smash against the side of the hotel, now as he looked out in the moon light, he had an excellent view of the boar. The thing stood in the moon light in front of the hotel, it was as big as a rhino easy just like that damn movie, its tusks were huge sharp savage things, and they could easy kill a man. Its eyes were like dark pits of hell in the semi darkness as it stared at the hotel. It was an image from a horror movie; he shook his head in disbelief.

The thing flew at the front of the hotel, and he heard the crash as the porch and front door caved in under the weight of the huge beast. He picked up his mobile and punched in the key the phone rang, "Hunter, I need you at the hotel now," he screamed into the hand set.

As Andy and Dave reached the top of the stairs the beast reached the bottom, the two men looked down in horror at the sight that met their eyes.

"Fucking hell," Dave said in disbelief.

"Let's get the fuck out of here," Andy said but he couldn't take his eyes off the beast.

The boar was panting as it looked up the stairs at the two humans, man would pay it had that one thought only. As the two men watched the huge thing pushed its large body up the stair way, the banisters broke and flew off in all directions as the beast moved quickly up, almost too big to fit on the stairs.

Andy ran for it and left Dave standing there the thing didn't pause and pushed its tusks into Dave's legs, he screamed as the beast smashed him against the back wall. Dave began to punch the beast on the head with his fists, crying out in pain as he did so, and the beast shook its massive head and Dave came free and flew across the landing. The boar went after him; his legs were crushed and bleeding badly from the two gaping wounds. The boar stamped on the man's belly hard and blood rushed out of the man's mouth, he lay back clocking on his own blood.

Brian heard the screams and got out of bed, he began to dress, and Julie got up with a start, "What the hell."

"Be quiet," Brian told her putting his finger to his mouth, "Get dressed and be quiet."

Julie began to dress, she moved to the side of Brian, "I think Dave is died I heard him scream."

Julie sobbed, "What is it."

"Just stay quiet Diny and the thing will go way."

Julie nodded tears running down her cheeks.

Andy ran down the corridor and came to the window at the far end; he tried to pull the window up the thing was stuck fast. He looked behind him, he could hear Dave's screams then he went quiet, as he looked, he saw the beast move into his line of vision. He heaved with all his might, the window would not budge it was no good, he had to get away.

He took a few steps backwards and looked round at the beast, the beast moved quickly towards him, Andy threw himself at the window. He crashed through the glass and went sailing into the night air, he screamed as the ground rushed up to meet him. He hit the ground hard, falling on a piece of jagged wood from the broken porch, it went through his neck and killed him at once, blood sprang from his neck like a fountain, splattering the front of the broken hotel.

The boar stopped before the broken window, the man had escaped it but he would not go far, the boar had smelled the two humans in the room as it had raced past. Brian sat on the edge of the bed with Julie, she was silently crying, he held her in his arms. They had heard the thing rushing past whatever it was the thing was big, and then the smashing of glass at the end of the corridor; Andy must have made a jump for it, good idea. As Brian stood up the door caved inwards, and the beast flew into the room like a bat out of hell.

Broken bits of wood went into Julies face and she screamed as she put her hands over her face, Brian was looking at the window as the door caved in; he twisted his head round and saw the beast, it crashed into his body. The beast kept on running and it dragged Brian in front of it and they both went crashing into the bathroom beyond.

Brian's body smashed into the bath, cracking the hard metal of the bath tub, his broken body fell to the floor as the beast stopped, and blood was pouring from its head from a wound caused by the wood from the door.

Its blood splattered the white floor as it turned and moved back into the bedroom, the room was empty, and it heard the human running down the stairs. It felt weak all of a sudden, the head ache growing worse, then a figure appeared at the broken door to the room, it raised something in its hands.

Hunter raced into the broken hotel; whatever had caused the damaged at the front was bloody big he thought he saw the woman on the stairs, blood run down her pretty face, "Get out quick."

He grabbed her and almost pushed her down the stairs; the beast had left the village alone, and come to the hotel looking for its meal he thought. The girl sobbed as she reached the bottom of the stairs, she turned and made her way out of the hotel, Hunter went up the stairs two at a time. He almost ran into Martin at the top of the stairs, the two men didn't say a word as Hunter lead the way down the corridor.

Hunter stood in the door way of the room, the huge wild pig faced him, he could see blood pouring out of a wound on its large head, and he raised his rifle. The beast turned to the window and as Hunter shot the beast twice in its side the thing crashed out of the window taking a large chunk of brick work with it as it went. Hunter and Martin looked down through the broken wall, the beast lay on its front on the ground, and then it slowly began to move, getting to its feet.

"Let's go Martin I hit the thing twice."

The boar was wounded badly as its body crashed to the ground, blood now poured out of its side as well, it would not die here, the huge beast slowly got to its feet, and moved off into the night.

8

Martin and Hunter followed the beast into the woods, it was easy to keep track of the beast was slow, and looked as if it was dying from lack of blood. Every stepped they followed they saw the things blood it was like leaving a crumb trail for them to follow. The beast went into the mountains the men close behind, the two men had been in this part of the mountain, they followed it then the beast disappeared. They followed the blood track with Hunter's torch and it led them to the cave, they must have walked right past this the other day.

"I'll be damned we must have walked right past this," Hunter said echoing Martin's thoughts.

"Yes," Martin looked at the entrance how badly was the beast hurt would it still have enough to attack them.

Hunter moved towards the cave, "Let's take it easy okay."

Martin nodded his head, "No worries their mate."

The two men entered the dark cave the torch light hitting the rock walls as they moved into the larger chamber, the beast lay on its side, its huge belly lifting up and down slowly. It was panting for breath, the two men saw the dead bodies that littered the cave, some were bones others half eaten corpses.

"Holy shit it must have been feeding on people for years," Martin said in wonder.

Hunter nodded, "Yes and it would be easy, a lot of people go missing here and no one reports them, it's a small place with small villages."

"Are you going to kill the beast while it's laying there", Martin had a feeling that the beast would jump up at any moment and kill them both.

Hunter shook his head no, "It's almost dead let it die in its home."

The beast let out a long sigh and its belly went still.

The paper factory just up river from the cave where the two men saw the beast die was working as always, the place was active twenty-four hours a day. There was a lot of paper needed in India as most of the work done at offices and such still used paper work, India wasn't open to the computer age as of yet. Offices would have piles upon piles of paper work stacked right up to the ceiling; some even had paper stack corridors you had to walk through to get to the desks. Yes, the paper mill made a mint producing its paper for the country, and India had no real environmental laws as such and so the paper mill got rid of its waste into the river.

The toxic paper waste would be pumped into the river day and night.

The female boar returned to the cave by the river bed, the water tasted bad today, she had managed to kill a small water rat, and held it between her teeth. She looked at her two piglets, they had woken up as she had come into the cave, she let the rat drop from her jaws and the bigger of the two piglets pushed its brother out of the way.

The piglet began to feed on the rat ripping it to pieces in a matter of seconds, the piglet was hungry and the aching inside its head had been annoying today. The young piglet was the size of a Jack Russell already and towered over its small brother. (2012)

The End

TWO

Night Bee's

1

The storm raged on during the night, the trees in the nearby forest swayed this way and that; some of the small tree's were pulled up out of their roots and thrown across the fields. This was the worst storm for many years in this part of England; the Kent country side had not recorded such a storm for decades. The bee hives stood firm against the storm in the field close to the forest, the rain lashed down on them in buckets, but not even the might wind could dislodge the hives.

The power cables in the next field supported by wooden pylons suddenly snapped under the pressure of the wind, the old wooden pylons had not been replaced for many years and were old. The power cables came down into the field where the bee hives stood, a massive electric shock went right through the ground, and trees at the start of the forest began to smoke. The Bee hives took the full might of the electric shock, and they seemed to glow in the dark as wave after wave of electric went through them.

2

The man whistled as he stood next to his Bee hives the power had been cut during the night god knows what damage the electric had done to his Bee's. He had to admit he was expecting a dead bee hives all round, he had twenty in all. It was going to cost him a lot of money to rebuild his hives again, but the bloody electric company would pay for that he would make sure.

Clive Banbury was forty-seven years old, but with his grey hair and beard looked ten years older, he had a pleasant face, round and jolly looking, he was overweight but didn't really care; he enjoyed his food and his beer. He looked across his field and saw the power cable lying inside just over by the stone wall.

Damn them he thought that silly old wooden pylon should have been replaced years ago; he now saw the broken pylon almost cut in two by the force of the wind. He went over to the first hive and put his hand on the lid, he held his breath and slowly opened it up, he looked inside and gasped in wonder.

The bees were sluggish but incredibly they were still alive, he couldn't believe his eyes, maybe they would pull through after all. He moved over to the next hive, it was the same the bee's seemed okay but just slow as if they were stunned, he moved his way down all twenty hives, and at the end zone he smiled. It was as weird as hell, but he was not going to lose his bees.

3

A week later Clive stood and watched as the power cable men went about their jobs of fixing the new steel pylon. It always took an accident of some kind before things would be changed it seemed to be the way of the world. He had been worried about his bees all week, they had failed to show at any time, and now he had to admit that maybe they wouldn't survive. He opened the lid of the nearest hive and looked inside; the bees seemed to have moved closer to the bottom of the hive, a few were at the top.

Then something strange happened, when the sun light touched the bees on top they began to blacken and smoke, then the bees caught alight. Clive slammed the lid shut, "What the fuck," he said out loud. He leaned against the hive, what the hell was going on, bees didn't just burst into flames when the sun light hit them, one word went into his head but he dismissed it straight away, 'vampire bees.'

No, it was something to do with that damn electric shock the bees had received, he looked at the workmen and gritted his teeth. He would give the electric company a piece of his mind;

he left the field and headed towards his cottage just over the wall
at the far end of the field.

4

That same night a strange sound could be heard coming from the
hives, the bees were buzzing once more and they sounded very
active. Suddenly dark clouds rushed up into the night air as
hundreds of thousands of bees emptied from the hives. It was
like a black carpet covering the black night sky, they buzzed
along blocking out some of the clouds as they went on their
way.

Colin was having so much success on this night, his right hand
now lay on his girlfriend's left breast, and boy did it feel so
good. He had taken his mother's mini clubman car; it was small
but hell what did he care he was going to get laid in it. He
rubbed the erect nipple and sighed this was going to be heaven,
he had been going out with Debbie for three months now and
had not so much as a blow job.

But now she had softened to his touch and he made her feel his
erection through his trousers, "Oh my it's so hard," she
whispered in his ear as he fondled her breast.

They were both eighteen and had never had sex, but they didn't tell that to each other of course that would be so uncool. Now he put his left hand up her tight little skirt, he felt her cotton panties and she let out a gasp. He put his hand inside her panties and could feel the hair of her fanny. Something brushed against his face, a bloody insect, "Fuck off," he shouted out.

"What," Debbie asked him.

"No not you a bloody insect."

Then another brushed his face and then he heard Debbie cry out, "There are loads of the bloody things," as she began to wave her arms about the cramp interior of the car. The bees swarmed into the tiny car, a window had been left open, and the bees were angry and confused as to why they could only come out at night, they stung the two mercilessly.

The infant school was having a sleep over and the teacher Harry Kent looked on with a smile, twelve children had been allowed to stay the night, and already the fun had begun. They had played apple bobbing and pin the donkey's tail and now they were getting ready to play musical chairs. The twelve six-year-olds looked at the teacher, he stood with a compact disc player in his hand, "Get ready," and he called out to them.

Harry was thirty-two years old and loved being a teacher, he was a gay man and no one knew of his private life at the school, and he liked to keep it that way. He knew that the school wouldn't do anything, but he had to admit that he liked some of the attention he received from some of the women teachers so he liked to pretend for now that he was a straight guy. God forbid if any of the teachers ever saw him at the local gay club, he went there every Friday and Saturday, and more often than not he was in a dark corner kissing some man he had met. But this night was the children's and he played the compact disc, and the kids ran around the chairs. He stopped the music, and poor little Lucy was left standing she began to cry.

"Never mind Lucy we will play again after this okay."

She smiled up at him and nodded her head; she was so cute with her ringlets in her golden blonde hair.

Lucy sat down by the open window and let the cool breeze wash over her face, she looked down at her hand resting on the window ledge, and a bee had landed on the back of her hand. She giggled even she knew that bees didn't come out at night time, "Sir," she put up her hand.

Harry looked round at her, "Sir a bee has landed on my hand."

He laughed, "Don't be silly Lucy you will get another chance to play in a minute."

Another bee came through the open window and landed on her neck this time the bee stung her she cried out in pain, and wacked the bee away from her. Harry turned at the cry and saw

Lucy moving away from the window, he couldn't believe his eyes as he saw a wave of bees come through the open window. He moved quickly and ran for the window, bees were all around him as he fought to close the window, and he managed to close it, but had been stung many times.

He felt dizzy but quickly shouted at the children; some of them were waving their arms about, "Get in the cupboard now."

The cupboard was a large area that went back five feet to a brick wall, and there wasn't much stuff inside it would serve them well, and they could kill the bees under the light. The children moved and so did he, he opened the thick wooden door and the children ran inside, the bees followed as well, but there weren't that many of them, he had saved the day by closing the window. He moved inside and closed the door, inside the cupboard the children started to kill the bees with the help of their teacher.

5

Next day the police called Clive he was the only bee expert around this area, he was drove there in silence in the police cruiser. As he got out of the cruiser, he saw the two black body bags and gulped, "shit man I've never seen a dead body," he had gone white.

Police inspector Jimmy Tibbs put his hand on the man's shoulder, "Please sir we just need to show you."

The body bags were unzipped and pulled aside, the face of the young woman was horribly disfigured and bumps were all over her face and puss oozed from some of the wounds, but there was no doubt that it was bee stings.

"Yes, that's bees alright inspector."

The inspector nodded and the body bags were closed once more, the inspector was a tall man and towered over Clive he rubbed his chin, "This happened last night sir."

Clive looked at the handsome face and said, "Excuse me."

"I know it's crazy sir but this happened last night."

"My bees have been acting strange since the electric cable juiced them up a few weeks ago."

He paused thinking "Maybe we should have a look at my bee's inspector."

A young policeman came over, "Sir we have just had a call about an attack on a school."

"Good god not bees again."

The young policeman nodded, "Yes sir but no one was killed save for a lot of bee stings."

Clive took the samples back with him; the inspector would be over just as soon as he had paid a visit to the school. Clive found some dead bodies in the hives, he had checked all twenty hives as soon as he got back, and they were all empty. He looked closely at the dead bees under the microscope, the bees had mutated into some kind of night insect. The bristles were dark black and the eyes seemed to have covers over them as if to protect from any light. The dead bees at the scene of the killings and the dead bees from the hives matched, the killer bees were his bees.

The inspector stood by the empty hives and sighed the school could have been a second killing scene, but thank God for the fast-thinking teacher.

"They are all empty sir," he said to Clive standing just over from him.

"Please inspector call me Clive and yes every single hive is empty I checked."

"Okay call me Jim."

He rubbed his chin it was a habit that he could never get rid of, "How do we find and destroy these bees Clive."

'I have an idea on how to destroy them they hate the light, blow them up in a ball of light killing the ones that try and get away."

"That's no problem but of course we have to find the damn things before night fall," the inspector said back to him. Clive sighed and nodded it was going to be a long day and he said to Jim, "We must check out all caves any where that's dark that might hide a few hundred thousand bees."

6

The next night Clive and Jimmy patrolled the streets of the city, it was a small city compared to London about the size of Norwich with a long shopping centre and lots of shops lining the walk ways. Clive had a canister of dye on his lap, he had thought of the idea earlier if they could find the bees at night then they needed to spray them, and then follow the track to their hideout. A simple plan but brilliant even if he did say so himself, they stopped at the MacDonald's and Jim opened his door, "Let's grab ourselves a burger mate."

Wayne looked across at the woman, she was okay not bad looking a bit too old for him, but she would serve her purpose tonight. He had hired the woman as an escort, it was the only way he could deal with women, he had never had a girlfriend they scared the hell out of him. But this way he was in control and that suited him fine, as long as he could just use a woman for sex, and then kick her out he was fine.

He looked around the posh restaurant, probably the best place she had ever been too he thought, but then he was rich so he could afford it. He was living on his mother and fathers allowance they would never let him work, no not their boy. He cut into the tender steak and could hear the woman talking about something, he wasn't interested, he just wanted to eat and then shag the brains out of her.

There came a cry from across the restaurant, he looked up and saw a, man doing a silly dance, he laughed out loud at the sight and looked at the woman she had her hand over her mouth. He looked again at the man doing the silly dance and saw that in fact he was surrounded by insects, bees to be exact.

The bees hit Wayne hard in the face, a blanket of them, he pulled his face back and screamed, the things were stinging him, he felt the pain again and again, he stood to his feet he could hear the woman screaming in front of him, but he couldn't see. The bees attacked and the people inside the restaurant didn't stand a chance, after the people lay still the bees exited through an open window, and out into the night.

Outside of the restaurant Clive and Jim stood back as the bees came out, they had got the call five minutes ago, the posh restaurant on 'Wood Street' was under attack, they had rushed over at full speed with the siren flashing. Clive pressed the nozzle and began to spray the bees as they came out, this seemed to put the bees off and instead of attacking the two men they flew off into the night sky.

"Thank fuck for that," Jim looked as white as a sheet.

"I got them good now to follow them."

Jim nodded he had thought they were goners for sure.

7

After a helicopter had been following the glowing mass all night the two men and some army guys ended up on the banks of a river not far from the city. Hidden in the dense trees there was a cave and it was this that the bees had flown into, the helicopter had radio it in and left the scene, now it was their job. The army men stood outside and it was agreed that Clive and Jim would enter the cave, and plant the explosives. Clive pulled on the thick white suit as did Jim besides him, they were both looking worried.

"Will the bees still attack in the day light," Jim asked Clive.

"I really wish I knew Jim this is a new breed of bees."

"Oh, okay mate," Jim answered looking more worried than ever.

"Maybe in a dark cave they can still attack I don't know."

Jim put on the helmet and said, "Well looks like we are going to find out soon enough."

Clive nodded his head and put on the helmet, it had a glass front and inside the head was a mike so the two men could talk. The army men watched as the two white suited figures entered the cave and disappeared, they had their guns at the ready.

There was a shorter tunnel as they entered, this was high but not very wide, the two men carefully walked down the tunnel it was pitch black, and the two strong torches cut through the darkness.

"Damn it's like a tunnel in here," Jim said waving his torch about.

"Yes, it is at the start, but I bet it opens out farther down into a large chamber."

The two men walked on, it reminded Jim of the time he had gone to India on holiday to a place called Ooty a hill station in southern India. They he and his mates had gone to the lake, after a go on the paddle boats they had checked out the house of horror. It was funny because outside the house of horror there was a box high up with a dummy mans legs hanging out and every now and then the thing would move. Inside the house of horror, it had been so dark that you couldn't see where you were going, and he had kept bumping into things that's what this tunnel reminded him of. All of a sudden, the torches swept round a large chamber just as Clive had said.

"Wow holy crap," Jim let out looking around the chamber.

In the torch light a few bees hovered about, "There are bee's men," Jim almost cried out.

"It's okay Jim don't worry the main nest must be sleeping."

"But where."

"Let's take a look up ahead, but first lets plant some of these explosives."

The two men set to work, and began planting the explosives in the large chamber.

"Got to make sure there is no back way out," Clive said pointing to another chamber which leads off from this one.

The two men walked into the other chamber and stopped the whole of the walls were covered in bees; the floor and ceiling were also covered in the things.

"Fuck me slowly," Jim said in a whisper.

The bees couldn't hear their voices inside the suits but Jim didn't know that.

"This is it then Jim."

"How the hell do we plant the bombs the bloody things might wake up?"

"Very true my mate."

Clive knelt down and planted a bomb at the start of the chamber.

"Plant the bombs round the entrance it will bring the whole damn cave down any way."

Jim nodded and began to plant all of the bombs round the second entrance. Clive looked about the chamber and said "There are no exits looks like it's just the one."

"Good stuff," answered Jim he looked at his arm as the last of the bombs were planted, there were lots of bees on his arm and now he could sense them on his back as well.

"Shit man the bees have woken up."

Clive had already seen this he moved his hand to his belt and removed the canister there, he opened the nozzle and smoke began to spill out. He smoked himself and then Jim the bees fell off the two men's suits.

"Right let's move," Clive said the bees had begun to wake up and there was a cloud of them close by.

The two men began to run for the tunnel, bees followed them; Clive kept turning and smoking the cloud of bees.

The two men entered the tunnel and made their way quickly through it, bees followed but they seemed dazed as if still half asleep. The two men came out of the cave and the army men rushed over to help them, they were pulled over to a clearing, bees poured out of the cave.

"Hit the button," Clive screamed as his helmet came off, the army man needed no second invitation.

The cave blew up from the inside and then a rush of hot air and a blast of dirt and rock as the entrance to the cave erupted and then collapsed and the cave was sealed. The bees that had come out with them soon hit the ground dead as the sun light smothered their tiny bodies. (2013)

The end

THREE

Good dog

The old man pushed a branch away from his face and went forwards into the forest following his beloved dog, George. Ernie Harris was sixty-two years of age and he had George for twelve years, and they had grown inseparable. He had white hair which was still thick on his head, his clean-shaven face was smooth and he looked ten years younger. He had only been married once and that was to a lovely woman called Betty.

Sadly, she had died five years ago and since that time he had relied on George to keep him company, he could hear George barking up ahead. He moved into a clearing and saw George barking at the ground, as he moved closer, he saw the snake, its body had been crushed. Ernie patted George on the head, "Good dog," the dog had bitten the snake, it was an adder and not that dangerous, but it was the only poisonous snake in England.

Just then he heard more voices coming this way, it sounded like kids, he waited with his dog and saw the tree's part and two tall young men walk into the clearing.

"Hello lads," Ernie said to the two young men.

Dave Anderson looked at the old man standing there with his dog he was twenty-one, and had an ugly spotty face. It looked as if grease lived in his very skin and his black hair was oily too swept back in a Robert DeNiro style.

"Fuck off," was all that Dave said to the old git.

Larry Parker was just as tall as Dave and he had his hair tied back in a pony tail, but he was a good-looking boy with a good smile and a pointed face, but this by no means made him ugly, his sharp features had won many a girl's heart.

"Yeah, fuck off you off cunt," Larry part in.

The two young men starred at the old man then Dave took out a hand gun. He had stolen it from his old man, and he and Larry were in the woods to do some target practice. Ernie saw the gun "Hey you guys come on be nice."

Dave pointed the gun at the old man, "All your money now."

"I haven't got any money young man."

"Don't you fucking lie old man," Dave waved the gun at the old man.

The old man held out his hands and said, "I'm walking my dog why would I need money."

"Come on mate lets go," Larry pulled at Dave, and Dave shrugged him off. He pointed the gun at the dog sitting by the old man's side and pulled the trigger. The dogs head exploded in a shower of blood and brains, the old man's legs were covered in the gore, he cried out in agony at the loss of his dog. He fell to his knees and held the dead dog in his arms, he cried out again and looked at the two kids, "You will pay for this."

The two men laughed and began to walk away, "Fuck you old man," Dave shouted back at him and then they were gone.

==

The old man sat in his favorite chair; he had just finished a hearty meal and was feeling very pleased with himself. George had come back to him, and that pleased him more than anything in the whole world, he stroked the air by his side and said, "Good dog."

He looked out at the night through the window from his chair, "It's time to go get those two critters George."

He laughed he could see George's tail wagging, he patted the air once more, "Good dog."

He had buried George that afternoon, taking the body all the way home in his arms; he had been tired by the time he had finished, and had gone inside his cottage and fallen asleep. Before falling asleep he had phoned the sheriff and told him about the two boys, in hind sight he wished he hadn't now but too late. He had awoken to panting by his side and he had been over the moon when he saw George lying next to him in the bed, the dog's favorite spot.

==

Dave watched the car drive away, thank fuck for that his parents had gone out for the evening, he was so pissed off with them all they said to him, was why don't you get a job always bumming around. And then the favorite one you can't live with us at home all your life you have to go out into the world on your own and grow up. Fucking cunts he gripped the hand gun in his hand, one day very soon he was going to waste his parents just like he did to that mangy mutt today.

His parents were well off and the house was built on the side of the hill, it was a luxury place and the garage had room for six cars, but he wanted everything for himself and soon he would be a very rich young man. He just had to get the timing right and make it look like a break in, boy he was going to enjoy seeing their brains splatter on the walls. He needed a fag, he drew the sliding French window and stepped out onto the balcony, the night was warm and he leaned on the rail looking down onto the tops of the trees down below.

He took out a packet of cigarettes and lit one; he inhaled the sweet tobacco and rested their closing his eyes. He heard the patter of feet behind him, he turned round it had sounded like a dog, but there was nothing there. He laughed killing that damn dog today had made him jumpy; it was only a fucking dog any way who gave a shit. He leaned on the rail again and looked down into the valley; he heard the patter of feet behind him.

This time he stayed where he was, the sound stopped right behind his back, then he felt an immense pressure on his back and cried out as the rail broke. The boy tired to grab thin air as he plunged down into the valley the tree tops rushing up to meet him.

==

Larry kissed the girl besides him, she was sitting in the passenger side of his mother's car, and he had borrowed the car for the evening his mum had said fine. He didn't have money like his mate Dave, but at least he got on well with his parents and they always bent over backwards to try and help him. The girl moved away and sniffed, "What's up babe," he said to her.

"God that smells," she said holding her nose.

He was so concentrating on his boner that everything else ceased to matter to him as his sense came back to him, he could now smell the smell and it was bad.

"I'm going," the girl pushed open the door and walked out closing the door behind her, fuck her thought Larry as he watched her walk up the street.

Plenty more fish in the sea, but that smell was bad it was coming from the back seats. He turned on the over head light and looked into the back seat and froze, there sitting on the back seat wagging its tail was the dog from the woods, its head was missing and blood pumped out of the stump. The wagging tail wacked against the leather of the back seat.

Larry screamed like a little girl and pissed his pants the dark stain appearing on his brown trousers, he opened the door and jumped out of the car, he fell to the ground. The dog followed him out and blood pumped into the air and landed on Larry's face, he screamed again as he tried to wipe away the blood from his face.

A woman pulled back her curtains and looked out at the scene on the street, some young fool and fallen out of his car. He seemed to be trying to get away from something, only there was nothing there only the drug crazy youth.

Larry ran down the street on wooden legs, he kept falling to the ground, his hands were bleeding from the falls and he looked behind him, the headless dog followed at a leisurely pace seeming to take its time. He screamed and ran out into the road, a car which had been speeding down the road crashed into him, he sailed over the roof of the car and landed in an untidy heap on the road, blood pooled around his head.

The car didn't stop and soon the tail lights disappeared into the night, the young man was unconscious but alive. Then as if something were put over his nose and mouth he began to choke and struggle as he tried to draw in breath. His body went still and the soft patter of paws on pavement receded into the night.

It was a strange case to be sure, and it still bothered Sheriff Hillman to this day, it had been three weeks since the two boys had been killed. Both of course looked like accidents, but the cases bothered Hillman as he sat at his desk, it was the weirdest shit he had ever come across. He had interviewed the old man of course he had been the one who had phoned it in about the two boys killing his dog.

Of course, the gun they found at the Andersons boys place had been confirmed as the gun which killed the dog. It was strange but they had found paw prints in the dust on the balcony, and the rail was strong how the hell had the boy managed to fall through it. The old man knew nothing and he was clearly not involved the crazy old fool kept saying that George had dealt with the two critters. It made him shiver George had dealt with the two critters, then the Parker boy's death, an old woman had seen him screaming and trying to get away from thin air saying she thought he had been on drugs.

There were no drugs in his system and they had found paw prints in the back of his mother's car and the doctor had said that something suffocated him; the head wound would not have killed him. He had thought of the old man, but he was in the clear no one had seen anyone or anything around the Parker boy that night. It was some mighty weird shit all right Hillman thought as he put his feet on the desk, and put his hands behind his neck.

==

The old man tutted as he looked out into the night from his kitchen, it looked like snow was on the way better get more logs for the fire.

"Don't want to get cold do we George," he said into the empty kitchen.

He turned off the gas and began to cut up the steak it was George's favorite. He placed the steak into the dog bowl and set it down on the kitchen floor. He patted the air above the dog bowl and walked into the living room; he sat down and turned on the television. He heard the dog bowl moving around on the kitchen floor and smiled, George so loved steak. He heard the patter of paws and waited for the dog to rest by his legs, he reached down and patted the air and said, "Good dog." (2013)

THE END

FOUR

Space spiders

The figure of the man floated past the window, he moved his arms as if swimming, and he floated over to a bench, and took a wrench from the top. He had been working on the new space station for a few years now, soon it would be George's time to go back to earth, and he was working in a team of five men, Ray, Burt, John and Terry. The work was hard specially when there was no gravity up here, but he loved working on the moon and boy was he going to milk it for all it was worth when he got back to earth, he would be a minor celebrity.

He began to fix a large screw into the wall and just happened to look out of the window, he thought he saw a spider, but that was impossible. He looked again and saw that the black hairy thing clung to the glass, it looked like a spider but this thing had only one eye, it was as big as his hand. Then the spider dropped off the window, he had better tell Terry, old Burt was outside doing some work.

==

Terry saw George coming towards him and waved as hand at him, "hey man how are you today," he had missed breakfast this morning as he had slept late. He had found it hard at first to sleep being tied into a bed, but now he found it all so comfortable and sometimes he slept in the men didn't mind the boss sleeping in.

"Terry, I saw something outside."

George came to a stop in front of Terry, the boss had a tea pouch to his mouth, and he had warmed it up in the microwave.

"What did you see George."

"It sounds so crazy but I saw a spider, but not a normal spider."

Terry took out the tea pouch and rubbed his chin, "Okay tell me about it."

"Well, it was black like a spider but it had only one big eye and the mouth area instead of fangs had a long dart like thing attached to it."

Terry laughed, "Have you been taking anything."

"No way you know I don't do that shit."

"I know mate go and tell ray to get Burt back in just in case."

George nodded at his boss and floated off down the white corridor use the sides to propel himself along.

==

Ray was the youngest of the five-man crew at thirty-two and he was angry at being made to go outside, it was such a pain in the arse to put on the space suit, and all this crap about spiders. He looked at George as he put his helmet over his handsome face, he had a goatee beard and jet-black hair, next to George with his mop of white hair and wrinkled face he was a super star.

"Okay Ray let's move it on out."

"Yeah, let's go and do this," he sighed inside the suit.

John had come to see what was going on, he always wore a smile, and he looked a cheeky bleeder with his ginger hair and freckled face.

"So, you're really going out to rescue Burt from the killer space spiders," he let out a laugh.

"Fuck you ginger boy," said Ray, John was the second youngest at just a year younger than Ray.

Ray moved into the chamber and George locked it.

"So, you saw some spiders for real George."

George looked at the ginger haired man, "I saw them."

John nodded now was not the time for jokes.

==

Burt let out a curse he was the oldest on the team at sixty-one and he was as bald as a coot, but he was a big jolly man and was the joker of the pack along with ginger who was also a funny man. He cursed again this sheet fitting was not going back into place, it had taken him all morning just to get the thing off and now the work was done, and he needed to replace the bloody thing. He saw a black thing crawling up the side of the space station, "What the fuck is that," he said out loud.

He had never in a million years expected to see something living and moving outside of the space station. Then he saw another, they were big about the size of a man's hand, and they looked like god damn spiders, but there was something wrong, yes, they had one big eye in the centre of their heads.

"Fuck this I'm out of here," he dropped the sheet and it floated down almost touching the moon's surface, it sort of hovered just above it.

He turned and saw more of the spiders, he cried out and lost his footing on the side of the space station, he floated down to the sheeting. He touched down on the surface with his backside; the spiders moved in a line they were everywhere now.

They crawled over his suit, "You can't get in here you fuckers," he said to them.

He felt his suit rip as hundreds of tiny rods punctured his suit, the air from outside rushed into the suit and the pressure blew Burt's head up like a balloon. It exploded in a shower of blood and gore and the spiders hurried inside the rips to feed.

==

Ray held onto the rail that went around the space station and made his way round, "You see anything Ray," it was Terry from inside.

"Nope boss nothing so far."

He turned a corner and saw the missing sheet in the side of the station, "Hang on there is a missing sheet on the side."

'That must be the one he was working on have a look around that area."

Ray saw the missing sheet on the moon's surface and he also saw the body of Burt, the suit was a mess and he could see hundreds of forms crawling all over it.

"Fucking hell," he cried out and quickly made his way back round where he had come.

"What's going on ray?"

"Fucking spiders every where they killed poor Burt sir."

"Get the hell in now."

Ray didn't need a second invite as he made his way to the air lock he was followed by hundreds of spiders. He was in a panic and entered the air lock in a rush he hit the side and panicked, the spiders poured inside as he closed the hatch. He breathed a sigh of relief as the air rushed into the chamber, he took off his helmet and looked round the chamber, there were hundreds of the things. He lost the ability to scream as the spiders flocked over his standing body.

==

Terry made a mad dash away from the air lock as George punched the open; he had seen the spiders in the chamber and had made a run for it. He heard the screaming from old George as the spiders swept into the space station, he almost bumped into John as he came round a corner fast.

"What the fucks going on boss."

He saw the terror in his boss's eyes, "Its George he opened the hatch and let them in."

"George is as blind as a bat, but Let what in boss."

"The fucking spiders that killed Burt and Ray."

Terry looked behind him and pushed John out of the way, he was gone down the corridor. John floated there and looked on as hundreds of spiders crawled around the frame of the corridor and dropped onto him, he screamed.

Terry was mumbling to himself as he made it into the radio room, he had to let the ground station know what the hell was going on up here. There were no doors inside the space station all the rooms were open so it was easier to float from one to the other without opening and closing doors. He cried as the spiders spilled into the room, they crawled up the sides and hung from the ceiling, they covered the whole room, and he was left standing among them.

He looked down at his feet there was a tiny circle were the spiders left him standing, he looked at the covered ceiling and walls. It was deadly silent then as if on a command the spiders closed in on him from all sides, he managed one scream and then it was over.

Ground control had not heard from the space station for two days now, "Maybe the weather is causing the block," Trevor said he was second in command alongside Ernest.

"Yeah, maybe you're right, but I want to send up a team just to be on the safe side." (2013)

The end

FIVE

The dog's day

Outside in the cool night air the army base was as quiet as the grave; two men walked the length of the compound and back rifles over their shoulders. The base was in the desert not too far from the gambling city of Las Vegas, the heat of the day had evaporated into a cool evening breeze which the soldiers were glad of. Deep down below the surface of the compound two scientists in white overalls stood looking down at the dog, the Doberman pincher looked in great shape, its lean body and smooth glistering coat testament to that. The army captain smiled down at the dog and said, "Where are the other dogs, Bill."

Bill one of the men in white turned to the captain, he had pure white hair and his wrinkled face showed his sixty years.

"They are ready also Bob sir."

Bob the captain nodded, he stood just over six feet tall and with his large belly and bald head was an imposing figure. Alex the third man in the room was skinny and short with a wave of ginger hair; he moved off to a door and opened it. In walked two more dogs, a Jack Russell and an Alsatian, both looked again in great shape.

"Have you selected a town captain," Alex said looking up from the three dogs.

"Yes, it is all sorted out they won't know what hit them."

"I feel sorry for them," Bill said.

"Don't this is a major breakthrough, and we have to test it properly."

The captain looked down at the dogs, "They have all been injected with the nano's and the virus."

Bill nodded, "Yes sir the nano's have worked on the vocal cords and the virus is in place to recruit more dogs."

"Good."

Alex couldn't help thinking what they had created, the perfect dog, super fit and smart and with the ability to talk.

==

The night silence was broken by the rumbling of the army truck; it stopped about a mile outside of the small desert town of St Christopher. Captain Bob Holloway moved to the back of the truck with two soldiers, the soldiers lifted down the tail gate and Bill and Alex came out of the back, the three dogs followed them onto the warm desert floor.

"Okay men this is it have you told the dogs what their mission is."

Alex stepped forward, "Yes sir the dogs have been briefed."

"Good good," the large man rubbed his belly and looked towards the town in the distance.

"Let them go."

The dogs looked at one another and then looked at the bunch of humans, and without a sound ran off into the night towards the small town of St Christopher.

"You stay out there for a little while Max," the old man called out into the yard, the small terrier sniffed round the rose bush not taking any notice of its owner.

"I will let you back in a bit later," and the old man closed the back door.

St Christopher comprised of one main road which ran through the town for a couple of miles, there were a row of stores closed for the night, and various streets ran off the main road. Most of the houses were made out of wood, one or two dotted about were made out of brick, and there was a duck pond in the middle of the town with benches for people to sit on. The three dogs ran down the silent main road, The Doberman stopped he had heard the old man; he looked at the other two, "This way men."

They ran over to the house and ran round the back of the house; the Doberman stopped and looked into the back garden.

"Right Jack you go round the left side, Al you do round the right."

The two dogs moved off, the Doberman went down the middle of the garden and the terrier spotted him, and began to bark its fur rose on its back.

"Don't bark my friend," the Doberman said the terrier stopped barking and rolled its head to one side as if trying to hear the sound again.

"Yes, you have nothing to fear."

The Jack Russell and the Alsatian moved to either side of the small terrier, the terrier sat down and wagged its tail.

"Jack do the honors solider," the Doberman ordered him.

"Yes sir," replied the Jack Russell.

The Jack Russell began to lick the terrier on the mouth, the terrier licked him back, and then the Jack stepped away. The terrier lay on the ground and began to twitch and growl softly, it lasted for maybe five minutes the three dogs just stood watching. Then the terrier jumped to its feet and faced the Doberman, "Ready for your commands sir."

The Doberman nodded its head up and down, "Good solider follow us."

The dirt shabby dog moved through the bins, it was hungry and the damn fleas were eating it alive, it heard a noise over to its left and looked up. A large Doberman stood just off to the left of the bins, the stray looked up from the left-over chicken pie, the smell was so sweet, and the dog wondered for a second should it eat or face the large black dog.

The stray looked at the Doberman, the dog wasn't going to attack the stray was ready for a fight even if it meant getting hurt.

"Stop that my friend and join us," the stray rolled its head as if it couldn't make out what was going on, the dog had spoken. The Doberman moved over to the stray it had an Alsatian by its side "Al now it's your turn to do the Honors."

The Alsatian moved over to the stray at first the stray growled at it, but then went silent as the Alsatian began to lick its mouth, the stray licked back. When the stray had recovered its feet the Doberman said, "First you get a bath solider."

The three dogs had gathered a small army by the time the town began to wake the next morning, walking behind the three was six soldiers.

==

The old man cursed again as he had his eggs and bacon in the small kitchen that damn dog had run away in the night. He had called the mutt in just before bed time, and there had been no reply so he had gone out into the back yard with a flash light no sign of the little fucker.

"Fucking dog," the old man shouted into the empty house, he walked with a limp, and he had a badly damaged knee from his school football days. It had been bad since when he had started all those years ago, but the coach had needed him so they kept injecting the pain killers. But of course, after a time the pain killers just made it worse and he had to quit early, he could have been a major league player but for that damn coach.

He moved off into the living room, he was now sixty-three and had lost all his hair years ago along with most of his teeth. He was a mean grumpy old man who only liked the company of his dog, and now that bastard had run away. There came a bark at the back door, the old man sighed and looked at the plate of eggs and bacon, "You be quiet you old mutt and let me eat."

Then under his breath, "Stay out all night you can stay out a little longer."

The dog barked again louder this time, the old man cursed and set the plate down on the small coffee table and rose to his feet. He limped over to the back door and opened it wide; he saw George sitting on the back door step behind him stood a huge Doberman, and an Alsatian.

"You brought friends home with you George."

"Yes, I have you old bastard."

The old man's jaw dropped open as he looked at his dog; it had just spoken to him.

"No way George you didn't speak," the old man backed away from the back door.

"You mean old bastard," George spoke again.

The three dogs padded into the house following the old man, the old man stumbled into the living room and fell into a chair. The dogs entered the Doberman in the lead, "Okay soldiers let's do this."

The terrier and the Alsatian jumped on the old man, he screamed as the terrier bit into his leg and the Alsatian started to bit his exposed neck. The feeble old man was no match for the super fit dogs and the mismatch lasted two minutes, the old man slumped dead in the chair, the Doberman ate the eggs and bacon and licked its lips, "Okay soldiers time for us to feed."

The army of dogs gathered at the back of the dinner. 'Wendy's diner' the sign had read out front. The back of the diner was in a narrow alley, wooden fencing blocking the view from the houses into the alley way.

"Okay men you hide, Jack and Al you stay with me."

The army of dogs hide themselves behind the large wheelie bins.

The Doberman could hear a human coming to the back door the smell of steaks was strong in the air, and it made the Dobermans mouth water, he had to feed his army before they took over the town. The man opened the back door and carried the bin over to the wheelie bins; he tipped the contents into it and turned back to the diner.

A large black Doberman stood in his way, "Get the fuck out of my way you mean looking mutt."

The man sneered at the dog trying to scare it away; he moved his arms and waved them at the Doberman, "Go on get."

An Alsatian and a small Jack Russell joined the Doberman all three dogs looked in excellent health, their coats shined in the light. The man hesitated, "What do you want boys," he looked from one dog to the other, "Want some food."

The man laughed, "Well you can fuck off I'm not scared of you lot."

But the man didn't move forwards, he was trying to convince the dogs and himself that he wasn't scared, but he was shitting his pants, these dogs especially that Doberman could rip him apart.

"Listen carefully and we will let you live."

The man sank to his knees and a wet patch appeared on the front of his white trousers, "Oh please this is not real," he must be hearing things or was it too much drink last night. He had told his mate Tony that he had an early start in the morning, but the fucker had kept buying the drinks, "Just one more for the road" he had kept saying.

"Get on your feet now," the Doberman ordered.

The man slowly got to his feet, "Please I will do anything just don't hurt me."

"I want you to go back inside and bring out nine steaks the biggest you got, and cook them I don't like raw stuff unless its alive."

The man giggled as the Doberman finished its sentence, "Alive" he said.

"That's right I only eat raw live things like you if you don't get moving."

The man starred at the Doberman, "You want nine big steaks."

From behind the wheelie bin stepped six more dogs all looked healthy as fuck "Damn bloody humans," said the stray looking at the man.

"Yes fuckers," said the small terrier, two boxers who were brothers looked at the scared man, and licked their lips together.

A mixed mutt which looked like a sort of like a greyhound but the head was all wrong, and then to make up the six a sandy colored Labrador.

"Man, it's going to be a big party," he giggled again.

"Move," the Doberman ordered.

The man moved past the dogs keeping his eyes on them all and pushed open the back door; the Doberman stepped forward and put its body in the way of the door so it couldn't close.

"If you try and run or tell anyone we will rush this joint and kill everyone inside including you, do you understand."

"Yes, I will tell my boss I have a big order to do now he will be cool if its money."

The food was excellent and the army feed well, the nine big steaks filled their bellies, the man was told to stand and watch. The Doberman finished first he looked at the short fat man in his white trousers and apron, "You are a piece of shit," the large dog hissed at him.

The man screamed as the large Doberman leapt upon him, he put his arms out to protect his face, the weight of the dog pushed the fat man over onto his back, his arms flew over his head and the Doberman bit down on the lily-white throat. Blood sprayed across the alley way and the other dogs looked on as their master finished off the fat man who had brought them food.

"Now the diner and don't spare anyone," the Doberman said to his army, the back door had been wedged open the pack of dogs ran into the diner, soon you could hear the screams from the people inside.

The man had managed to escape the carnage inside, but he was badly hurt, blood covered his face and hands, he collapsed on the fore court of Wendy's diner, he saw a couple of young men across the street.

"Help," he called out to them.

The two men stopped and looked at the bloodied man on the fore court.

As they looked the front window of Wendy's diner with the words 'free coffee with every breakfast, exploded outwards in a shower of glass. A group of dogs fell to their feet and one a boxer leapt on the bloody mans back, he screamed as another brown boxer helped in the slaying. The two men stood there and watched, rooted to the spot, a large mean looking Doberman jumped through the broken window and saw the two men.

"Hey fuckers," the dog shouted at them.

"What the fuck," said the shorter of the two men, his name was Danny and he was only in the town for the day visiting his mate Larry who stood beside him.

"Come on let's get the hell out of here," Larry pulled his mates coat but Danny didn't move, Larry ran off towards a high building.

It was the tallest building in the town and was a block of flats, thirty flats in all. Larry lived there and it was the perfect place to hide out in safety. Danny didn't move as the Doberman and an Alsatian leapt upon him, he cried out in pain and blood ran from beneath the two dogs as they savaged the man.

Amy and Rocky Hill had lived in the town their whole life; they were well up on what happened in the town. That day they had witnessed the pack of dogs killing folk in their town, when the pack had run over to the block of flats, they had made their move. The safest place in this town would be the church and already that day they had rung their friends and the priest and told them what was going on, of course they didn't know the dogs could talk. So that's where Amy and Rocky ended up inside the locked church with five other people including the priest father Moore.

The army of dogs couldn't get into the block of flats, the iron gates were locked and you had to have a key to open them, the Doberman listened there were not that many people inside the flats.

"Okay soldiers there are not many people in there," he looked over the town and his eyes fell on the old church.

"Let's go see what's happening in the church," the others followed as he darted away towards the church, they had not been on this side of the town so far.

The Doberman stopped and waited for this army to catch up, he could hear humans locked up inside, they thought they were safe but the windows with their lovely art work would be easy to break.

"We attack the church soldiers," he looked at the windows and the dogs understood.

==

Father Moore looked about the interior of the church, he was sitting on a pew near the back as was everyone else, and he was a tall thin man with grey hair receding rapidly. He smiled at Army Hill she was a good woman still good looking at fifty-five years younger than him, she dyed her hair black but it suited her pretty face. He looked at her husband Rocky now there was a character, he had been a professional boxer for a few years, but had suffered terrible cuts and had to quit. He looked like a boxer with his flat nose and the scar tissue over both eyes, and he hardly had any eye brows.

Then there were the Adams family, he nearly laughed but stopped himself he had been thinking of the old television show the Munster's. Terry Adam sat next to his wife Lucy, he was a short man about the same height as his wife and they were both fifty-three. Their two sons sat close by as always, they had never left the family home, a couple of wasters if ever there were. Both boys well not boys both were in their early thirties, they were fat and didn't work.

Jack the eldest had never worked in his life and Tony the younger one had only ever had a few part time jobs around town. Their parents had a bit of money from a long-ago dead aunt, and the boys were content to live off that.

Father Moore still wasn't sure if he were being put on about all this, a pack of dogs over running the town, and Terry claimed he had heard one of the dogs speaking. Surely not that was just ridiculous, he looked around the church, they sat near the two large doors at the back, there were twenty rows of pews leading up to the altar, a large statue of Jesus took centre stage at the altar.

The Doberman looked at his soldiers, it was time, he could hear the people inside the church talking, he took a long walk backwards, his soldiers followed. He looked at the church windows and tensed his lean body; he ran at the church and leapt at the stain glass windows. The other dogs followed suit and they seemed to jump in illusion, the silent night was shattered by the sound of braking glass.

He didn't know why or how but as soon as the glass windows shattered inwards, father Moore was on his feet and running for the altar. Beside the altar there was a door and through this door was his office, and in that office, he kept a drum of petrol. He saw the shiny bodies of the dogs as they crashed through the windows, broken glass flew everywhere, he ran as fast as his legs would carry him, thankfully the dogs seemed to ignore him and go for the others. He hoped that he could be quick and help save the rest of them, this was the only way the dogs would kill them all if he had just sat down.

Rocky punched the boxer that leapt upon him, the force of the beast knocked him to the floor, and he could hear his wife Amy shouting out in fear. Rocky held the dog in one arm and hit it again on the jaw, the dog lunged at him and caught his fist in its mouth, blood poured out as the dog bit down hard, Rocky screamed out in pain. Amy fell to her knees as the Jack Russell and the terrier jumped on her body, she tried to cover herself with her arms, trying to protect her pretty face.

The Jack Russell tore into her leg, she screamed in agony as the terrier took one of her arms in its mouth. Tony kicked out at the Alsatian he missed and fell backwards onto his fat arse the stray was on him in a second. Ripping out the fat boy's throat, blood sprayed onto his fat brother who was trying to crawl away on the floor. The Doberman jumped on the crawling fat boy, and the other boxer dog helped, they both began to tear the boy's clothes off, ripping into his fat white skin.

The Labrador had Terry on the ground; Terry was holding the dog by the scruff of the neck while his wife Lucy tried to kick the dog in the side. But the mixed Greyhound soon came to the Labrador's rescue and bit into the woman's calf and held on, she screamed and tired to get the dog off her, blood run down and pooled on the floor. It was almost a comical scene as the woman hopped about with this furry thing attached to her leg.

Father Moore came out from the room, he began to let the petrol run over the floor, he heard the screaming and could see the dogs over powering them all. He walked down the pews letting the petrol flow out, as he reached the carnage the Doberman looked up at him, the dog saw the can and ran to the windows.

"Quickly now everyone out of the windows," the priest stopped and looked at the talking dog, his mouth wide open in shock. It lasted a second and then he was throwing the petrol can at the dogs, he ran back a little and then flicked open his lighter. The Doberman was through the windows in a second, the other dogs were so intent on killing their victims they hardly heard their master.

The flames blew up and the church caught fire, Terry moaned as the flames lit his clothes he was not far from death, his two boys were dead and he couldn't see his wife. Amy starred at the ceiling with lifeless eyes; Rocky moved as the flames took hold, he pushed off the boxer dog, which now ran around the church with flames on its back. Rocky staggered to the large wooden doors at the back of the church and lifted the wooden beam that closed them; he pushed open the doors, and let in the night air.

The air rushed into the church and gave the fire extra fuel, the flames leapt higher, the dogs ran around blindly smacking into pillars and pews, "HELP," cried the stray its body engulfed in fire. The Alsatian made it outside the doors, its body badly burnt by the fire. Father Moore tripped as he ran into the church, the line of petrol he had laid beneath him, the flames rolled over him and he found his clothes alight; he patted his clothes with his hands.

Then the Labrador jumped onto his belly the wind was knocked out of the priest, the Labrador jumped off flames licking at its fur, and ran wildly about the church. The father laid down the wind out of his body then he felt himself being moved, he put his head up and saw Rocky pulling him through the flames to the back of the church. The Alsatian had gone passed Rocky and ran into the night. Rocky had seen the priest through the flames and had run back in to save him.

He saw the burning bodies of his friends and his wife, but he had to stay focused on rescuing the father. The two men lay on the grass outside the church, Rocky was bleeding from several wounds on his hands and arms, he also had burns to his face, the father was burnt on the face also and his hands. They lay there and hopped that someone would come to their aid soon, they didn't have the energy to move any more.

The Doberman looked back at the church, his army had failed they would all burn inside the church, as he was about to set off, he saw the Alsatian running into the night, fire and smoke coming from its back. The Doberman followed the Alsatian until the Alsatian fell to the ground, its back still slightly burning, the Doberman approached the dog, "Hey Al how are you."

The Alsatian looked at its master, "I'm hurt bad sir."

The Doberman walked over to his friend, "Do you want me to end it for you soldier."

"Yes, I am in so much pain please sir."

The Doberman tore into the Alsatians throat; the dog was soon out of its misery.

==

The Doberman ran out of the town and down one of the freeways, it soon saw the road block the army was waiting for him. He stopped at the road block and Captain Bob Holloway approached him, "Sir all of the others are dead."

"But did you complete the mission," Bob said rubbing his large belly.

"Yes, sir we took over the town, and could have killed them all in time."

Bob nodded the Doberman was told to go into the back of the truck; he would be feed and rested and got ready for the next mission. Bill and Alex strode up to the captain, "So it was a success in a way sir," Alex said his ginger hair looking dark in the night.

"Yes, the dogs would have taken over no doubt about that, but we put a time limit on this one so the town is lucky."

"But all the other dogs are dead sir surely it's a failure," Bill put in.

Bob looked at Bill then at Alex and said, "This is a great success the Doberman was a great leader and will be again soon the others were expendable."

With that the captain walked to the back of the truck.

The town folk who had survived were paid handsomely to keep their mouths shut, they didn't have much choice either take the money or end up in an army prison. The folk took the money as far as the press were concerned the town had a pack of wild dogs that had run amok and killed a few people, but the press soon lost interest after a few days, and went onto better news.

Father Moore used his money to rebuild the church, and make a nicer rectory for him to live in next to the church, he was worn out and tired, the talking dogs had really pushed him over the limit he wanted to forget and that's just what he did.

Rocky buried his beloved wife and took the money from the army, he hated them and knew it was all an experiment, but he played the part of a tired broken widow. He would use his money to get his own back on the army one way or the other, this matter was far from over as far as he was concerned. (2013)

The end

SIX

The new breed- spiders in India

The white man read his paper, he sat in a small coffee shop, he had arrived in the village of Latur that afternoon, but to call the coffee shop a shop was going a bit far, it was a tin hut with plastic chairs that had seen better days outside. The man read his paper while a few of the locals gave him funny looks; Anthony Leopard was an English man. He had been sent to Latur by his company to find the new breed of spiders, in the past five days several people had been killed in Latur by an unknown spider.

The witch doctors the so-called Hindi priests had been giving the victims herbal medicine, completely inadequate, but what did they know of the real world they lived in a third world country. It was the backwardness of the people and the so-called priest that would never make this damn country go forward.

Anthony was six foot dead and had sandy hair which was tied back in a pony tail, he was thirty-five years old and single, his work meant far too much to him to bother with women. He was thin and had a pointy face, but he was a handsome man. Now he had the chance to find and name a new species of spider, he hadn't been this excited since he had found a new breed of butterfly in Brazil ten years ago. But it was spiders that were his true love, he had studied them most of his life ever since he had been a kid and would watch the spiders spin their webs for hours, he would just sit and watch. He had once had a fight with a boy at school because the boy had stepped on a spider on propose, he had beaten the boy up, and it had given him great pleasure to avenge the killed spider.

He didn't know much about the spider apart from patchy stories, it was black and yellow and was the size of a man's hand, the bite was painful and the venom acted within seconds, blood coming out of every orifice. He had pin pointed the spiders down to an area which was only inhabited by tribes, it was way out in the sticks of Latur. He and his team of three others would start out tomorrow, for now he read his paper and relaxed under the watchful glances of the locals.

==

The man crept up to the tin hut, inside their lived a family, the parents were out tending their crops and had left the young daughter alone, the young man moved up to the tin hut and looked through a crack. He could clearly see the young girl, she was fourteen, and she was beautiful he thought to himself. The young man had never been to school he lived in a tribe, and they taught their own way of life to the youngsters. But Kople who was now sixteen had been having urges for a long time now and he wanted to see naked women, and lots of them.

The women wore sari's in his tribe, but not a lot else. He watched the young girl strip and started to wank his penis it was as hard as rock. Soon the young girl was naked, she had tiny breasts that stood upwards with pointy nipples, she had a black mound of pubic hair between her legs, this was too much for Kople and he came in a rush all over the back of the tin hut. He moved away from the hut now with a plan in his head, he would wait until the girl was sent out alone and he would follow her and then pounce, he wanted her badly now and nothing was going to stop him.

==

The man was sweating inside the tin hut; this one was just over the other side of the small village from the young girl's hut that Kople had been spying on. The man had two young boys, one boy was asleep on a bed of straw the other was playing with some sticks, pretending that they were men fighting; the little boy loved the tales of wars told by his father.

The man was alone his wife had been killed only days ago by a spider bite, it was a new spider no one in the tribe had ever seen one of its kind before. They had found his wife's body being dragged along the ground by the spiders, blood was coming out of her eyes and her ears it was a gruesome sight.

Something a spider never did, and they had stamped on them and killed them with spears until the spiders had left the body alone. They had burnt her body two days ago and the man was still trying to come to terms with her death, and how he would cope with his two young boys.

The boy who slept suddenly gave a loud moan, the man looked across at him, and the boy started to hemorrhage and blood poured from his eyes, his nose and ears, the man was on his feet in an instant, and told the other son to get out of the hut in Hindi. But the small boy was far too interested in seeing what had happened to his brother, the man picked up his now dead son, a spider fell to the ground.

It was pure black and had a yellow stripe going down its back, and it was big maybe the size of a large man's hand. The spider moved quickly and the man brought his foot down on soil, the spider ran up the man's leg and then he screamed out in agony. He dropped his son and fell to his knees, more spiders came into the tin hut, the other son was soon crying out in pain.

At this time the tribe village was quiet many people went to the fields to trend the crops, the army of spiders dragged all three bodies out of the hut, and slowly they made their way into the jungle of trees and bushes.

==

Anthony wasn't too bothered about the three men with him, he was in charge, and he let them know it. He wasn't out here in India to make friends, but the four white men were a strange sight in the small town of Latur. They began their journey into the dense forest that morning, there was Russell the largest man in the group at six three, he wore blue overalls as did all of them, thick overalls and boots and groves.

He was bald and had a large belly, he enjoyed his food and beer in England and didn't care who knew it, but he also enjoyed working for the company, he and the other two were what is known as clear up mess men.

The other two in the group had flame throwers on their backs just in case, Anthony carried a leather bag, he wanted live samples, the two men with the flame throwers were Pete, a short hairy man, he looked like an ape with his mass of brown hair and busy beard, and Jack a slim medium height man with blonde hair and glasses. The four men carried on, if the directions were correct, they should hit the village soon, word had reached the town that another family had been killed by the spiders the bodies were missing. Anthony was in a hurry he needed to see these spiders; he was excited he would name them after himself. Anthony spider no Leopard spider sounded better, he thought about this as they made their way through the forest.

==

The four young people were laughing as they made their way to the tribal village they were from the town and wore modern clothes, well as modern as they could be. They looked like something out of the seventies with their disco style shirts and faded black jeans, but compared to the tribe they were modern. Two men and two women, two of them were going out together the other two were trying to make up their minds if they could work out together; they had been friends for so long.

Rachel was a Christian who spoke good English as did the rest.

"Look at that," she said pointing; Martin who fancied her something bad, but was having trouble asking her out, they were the two who were trying to make up their minds about each other. She looked even more beautiful as she stood in the sun pointing at the ground, he followed her finger and saw the hole in the ground, and it was large, around the size of a large tractor tire. Susan and Ali stopped and also looked at the hole, they had been going out together for four months now, but he still hadn't gotten his end away, but he was hoping it would happen soon, last week she had allowed him to feel her breast.

Rachel and Martin moved closer to the hole.

"Hey guys I wouldn't go to near that thing," Ali called out to them.

"Rachel come on let's get moving."

They had come to the forest to see the village where all the spider deaths had happened, since the reports they had become interested, and when they got back, they could tell all their friends about it. It would make a good story to tell plus a few made-up things thrown in just to spice it up a bit.

As the two young adults went nearer suddenly the hole erupted into life, spider's large ones poured out of the hole and attacked the two youngsters, they didn't stand a chance. Rachel was bitten on her legs and fell face first onto the grass, Martin tried to beat the spiders with his fists. He managed to squash two of them, but he was soon over whelmed, as the other two starred in horror the bodies were pulled into the hole. Spiders began to walk quickly towards the two standing youngsters, Ali grabbed Susan's hand and they ran back into the forest.

==

Kople watched the four young people he watched the two in front, the girl had large breasts he could tell by looking at her top, he was hard and began to wank himself as he watched them. The other woman had smaller breasts, but she looked fitter and Kople bet that she had a black hairy fanny just like the young girl who he was going to fuck real soon. He was almost at the point of no return when the spiders came out of the hole. He stopped his wanking and just looked in horror as the two young people were attacked, and then dragged into the hole, the other two started to run for the forest.

Ali dragged Susan behind him and almost ran straight into the group of four men, two of the men had funny packages on their backs and held metal nozzles.

"Hey," the man with the sandy hair and pony tail said as Ali almost crashed into him. Ali stopped and got his breath back, "Spiders," he said looking back the way he had come.

"Show us," the man said to them in a gruff voice.

"Please sir they were chasing us."

They all looked back, but there were no spiders.

"They came out of a hole in the ground and took our friends," Susan sobbed at the men.

"They took the bodies into a hole."

"Yes, sir killed them and then dragged them into a hole," Susan replied.

"Amazing," said the man with sandy hair, he was quite good-looking thought Susan as she looked at him.

"Show us now," the man said again in a gruff voice that said you better do as I ask.

Anthony looked at the hole, amazing the new breed of spiders lived underground, he could see no sign of any webs, there should be some, maybe they didn't spin webs, this spider was getting more and more interesting by the minute, and he had to see one for himself.

"Okay you two cover me I'm going to look down the hole."

The two men nodded and followed the boss, he walked slowly looking at the ground in front of him, and he was hoping that the spiders would be busy with the two dead teenagers. He reached the edge of the hole and looked down, he could see the bottom it was about three feet down, and then a tunnel went underground to God only knew where, but the tunnel was also big, large enough to drag a human body into. There were no sign of any spiders as the two men with flame throwers reached the edge of the hole, Anthony scratched his hair now what to do, and he needed specimens.

Then he got his wish as one spider came out of the tunnel, it stopped there as if it could sense the men above it. Anthony looked at the new breed, it was pure black and had a yellow strip across its back, it was the size of his hand easy, and he could see the sharp fangs dripping venom.

He could also clearly see its four eyes, this spider had only four eyes it was amazing.

Then there were two and then three and suddenly the spiders poured out of the tunnel, Anthony reacted quickly he stepped back and said, "Torch them."

Pete was closest to the tunnel and he panicked when he saw the spiders, the edge of the hole crumbled and he lost his footing, he tried to turn on the flame thrower but slipped into the hole, he screamed as the spiders went en mass over his body.

"Torch the fucking things."

Jack needed no second command, he let the spiders have it, the flame shot out from the nozzle and he arc it all over the hole. Pete who was dead any way went up in flames; Anthony opened his leather bag and brought out a clear glass container. With tweezers in hand, he picked up a spider that managed to avoid the flames, he popped it into the container and then went around the burning hole; he found five specimens and was a happy man.

"Oh my god the smell," Susan said crying into her boyfriend's shoulder; he held her tight looking in horror at the burning hole.

"Fuck this Pete is dead man," the large man said, Russell didn't really like Pete that much, but fuck he was dead and they were out in the damn sticks.

"We carry onwards," said Anthony.

"There could be more holes, we have to kill the threat now do you understand."

He had his specimens now they had to rid the forest of this menace.

"But Pete is dead," Russell said in disbelief.

"Come on man snap out of it we have to save people's lives," Jack patted the big man on the arm; he nodded as if he understood.

"Come on let's find this village."

The man stopped and looked back at the two kids; he had almost forgotten about them.

"Go back into town and tell the police.'

The young man nodded and he took his girlfriends hand and disappeared into the bushes heading back to the town of Latur.

==

Kople watched the men and saw one of them die in the hole, the frames coming out of the nozzle fascinated him, and then he saw the two young people run for the town and the men head for his village. He had seen one of them holes in another part of the forest and he now made his way to it, he wanted to make sure then maybe tell the men, and again sees the flame come out. He stopped the hole was by a stream and now he could see a naked woman with her two young children.

She was bathing them and herself. She stood up to her knees in the water and as she turned, he could see her full nakedness. He saw the black bush of her fanny the small breasts and they were well shaped; he was hard in an instant, he took out his penis from his loin cloth and began to wank himself. The kids were far too small to be of concern for him, but the mother was gorgeous and he wanked himself hard thinking of entering hcr black fanny and thrusting away and then kissing her as he came inside.

He spurted his load over the forest floor, some of it hitting the spider which was watching him. He took one look at the spider with his semen on it and ran, the woman looked over to the trees and bushes she had heard a noise. Then she saw the spiders come out of the forest and into the clearing by the edge of the stream, there were hundreds of them and they were big, she picked up her two kids but the spiders stopped. They were waiting for her, they couldn't swim but they were waiting for her, she began to scream at the top of her lungs.

Kople ran into the village and saw the men, he pointed to the forest, and then they all heard the screaming. Anthony looked the boy up and down, he was only wearing a loin cloth, and the young boy was pointing into the forest.

"Come on men lets go."

The three men went into the trees then the young boy went in front.

"Okay men lets follow him."

Anthony was pleased the young boy had taken the lead now they would reach the spiders quicker, he could have got lost in these forests.

==

They came out into the clearing, Anthony saw the sari and small kid's cloths on the ground, he then saw the naked woman holding her kids in the stream, the sight was unbelievable the spiders were on the shore, and they were waiting for her. This new breed was altogether amazing and he couldn't wait to start opening up his specimens. He would keep two alive to breed of course, in his lab he would have a large containment tank built for them. Russell was losing it the sight of so many spiders just waiting on the shore sent him crazy, he turned and ran back into the forest.

"Hey Russell where the hell are you going," Jack shouted at his back.

The spiders turned as one towards the men, Jack got his frame thrower ready, and Anthony looked on in wonder.

'Leave him be," Anthony relied.

Russell just ran blindly into the forest, the trees were many and thick, he ran straight into one and hit his face full on the bark, he fell backwards half conscious. Blood poured from his broken nose and two of his teeth slipped out of his bleeding mouth. The spiders came out of the bushes and stopped for a second before the large bellied man, and then they slowly walked over his body as if they knew they had all the time in the world.

Russell didn't even scream as the spider's bit into his large body.

"Torch them," Anthony ordered as the spiders came towards them.

It was a massacre as the flame roared down on the horde of spiders, the burning black bodies began to sizzle and splutter as the flames hit them, the spiders retreated back into the woods but many of their number had been killed. The black oozing burnt bodies littered the shore line as the woman came out of the stream, Jack got her clothes and she started back to the village. Anthony had one last look at her lovely backside then she disappeared.

"Right now, we find the hole."

The boy was drawing something in the sand by the stream, Anthony went over and looked down, and it was a picture of a hole and an arrow pointing into the forest. The boy pointed and Anthony knew what he meant he knew where the hole was.

"Okay Jack it's me and you buddy."

He looked down at the sand and Jack done the same, the boy was heading into the forest looking back to make sure they followed; he didn't want to be on his own by the hole.

"Come on Jack let's go."

As they followed the boy through the thick vegetation the heat ever so hot all around them, it was like being in an oven inside the thick forest. They came out into a clearing and there was a little breeze that Anthony welcomed with open arms his blue overall was soaked. He saw the second hole in the ground it was identical to the first one, made exactly the same way.

"I torch the damned thing boss."

Before Anthony could answer they, all stood open mouthed and looked at the scene before them. On the other side of the hole the body of Russell was being dragged along the ground by a horde of spiders. As the men watched the spiders came to the hole and let the body drop in, and then all the spiders disappeared into the hole.

"Amazing," said Anthony.

"Amazing or not boss we got to torch the fuckers."

Anthony nodded his head, he hopped he had two different sexes in his containers, the odds had to be good.

"Torch them."

Jack went up to the hole and this time didn't wait for the spiders he torched the hole, aiming the flames into the tunnel at the bottom. Spiders tried to run out but were consumed by the flames it was all over in five minutes, the black hole smoked. The boy clapped his hands in wonder at the thing that spat flames.

==

Anthony was about ready to leave this place when he heard news of a new hole; about twenty feet from the last burnt one.

"Fancy one more job before home Jack."

He had grown to like Jack in the two days since the burning of the last hole. The two had even spent a night drinking in Anthony's room, the whisky was cheap in Latur and Anthony had a few bottles to take home as well. Latur was a god forsaken place, it was just a dirt town, everywhere there was dirt, the stalls were made from old metal taped together most of the time, ladies sold fruit and vegetables on the floor on cloth's laid out on the ground. Folk poured water over the dirt every few hours to stop the dirt rising, but that didn't help you always seemed to be coughing dirt in Latur.

The shops were just holes in the walls and where ever you went there seemed to be a cobbler on the ground waiting to repair your shoes. But it had been a good experience and Anthony was so pleased with his spiders, he had studied them through the clear glass, and had defiantly got two of each sex. He couldn't wait to start breeding them back in his lab, and learning more and more about them.

"One more job and that's it we get the hell out of dodge," Jack smiled at Anthony.

They had lost two good men on this trip and the company wasn't pleased, but when they heard of the specimens, they seemed to calm down a bit.

They approached the new hole this time they had three policemen with them and one of them was the chef. Anthony had promised them to leave the frame thrower for them when they left for England. But the chef had to come along with a few men so they knew what to look for if it happened again in the future. Jack walked up to the edge of the hole and looked down, it was all quiet and empty down there, apparently two more villagers had been killed last night, and their bodies had gone missing.

Jack torched the hole and aimed the flame right down the tunnel again spiders tried to run to the surface again but were burnt instantly. After a few minutes Jack stopped and the black smoking hole pumped its smoke into the air the smell was bad as well, and a couple of the police officers gagged.

"Well chief that's all it takes to wipe them out."

The chef nodded he could speak English, "Thank you so much Mr. Leopard."

Anthony walked away then stopped and turned to the chief and said, "By the way chief the spiders are called Leopard spiders."

==

Kople watched as the young girl moved through the forest, he had waited ages for this chance, and now at last they had let her go alone into the forest. She held a clay pot in her hands so she must be getting water from the stream, the father usually did this but he had looked tired after a day tending crops, Kople had been watching their tin hut for some time. He wanted the young girl badly and had dreamed of her every night for two weeks, since the spiders had been wiped out the village had returned to normal. He made himself wait until she had filled the clay pot and began making her way back to the village, he wouldn't harm her, he had made a mask for his face out of leafs.

As she walked past him, he leaped out from behind a tree, he caught her by the arm and she dropped the clay pot, it shattered on the ground and the water ran into the dry soil. He pulled her into the forest of trees, she would never tell her parents what had happened she would be too ashamed, he knew his and smiled, she would make up some other story.

He pushed her roughly to the ground and ripped off her sari, he ripped the top half off first and saw the pointy breast's he took one of them in his mouth and sucked hard, she moaned and tried to push him off her, but he was too much for her. She seemed to accept what was happening and didn't move, he removed the bottom half of the sari and saw the black bush of pubic hair he was so hard. He pushed his penis into her and started to thrust away, it felt so good.

He kissed her on the mouth and then gagged and stopped thrusting he had blood in his mouth. He looked down at her, blood ran out of her mouth and her eyes, he could see it running out of her ears at the side. He felt the first spider crawl onto his bare backside and cried out in terror. (2013)

The end

SEVEN

Death roaches

The white van stopped behind a block of apartments, most of the apartments were holiday homes, but still a few people lived there or rented out all year round, so the flats were always busy to some extent. The short fat man got out of the van and went round the back; he opened the double doors and picked up a flash light and a crow bar. The drain was next to the curb on a small road which led past the apartments, across the road on the other side were another set of apartments and a tennis court with a wire fence going round, the man could see a couple of old timers having a game.

Playing tennis in this heat and there was a bar across from the tennis courts called the 'rovers return' now that's where Paco would rather be any time of the day. He smiled they had to be crazy brits playing in the heat of Spain, crazy he thought to himself, he always took things so slowly like most of the locals. But back to work he inserted the end of the crow bar under the drain and lifted, it came up easily, and he laid it down on the ground, and then went back to the van.

He put a couple of cones round the hole and turned the flashing lights on at the top of each cone; he positioned himself and began to climb down into the sewer. The sewer company had some complaints about people dumping waste into the sewer, they had been seen several times, and the witness were not sure if they were doing it for the local chemical plant. There had been rumors for years that the chemical plant hired boys to dump their waste, but as of yet no one could prove it.

He reached the bottom Paco lit up a cigarette and thought about his wife, she was staying out late last week or two, and he was starting to think that she was having an affair. He would have to slap her around a bit soon just to put her back in her place.

They had been married for ten years now without children at forty-two Paco thought he would never have kids, but in truth it didn't bother him, this family loved kids, he didn't. No, his dog Jesus was all he needed, he cared for that dog even better than his wife, he was sure that she was jealous sometimes, well bollocks to her he admitted that yes, he did love the dog more so there, and one day he was going to tell her that.

He turned on the flash light and made his way down the tunnel, it was pitch black down here, he could hear a car running over the top of him, he heard a sound to his left and turned. He shone the flash light and saw a mass of moving insects; there were thousands of the things running across the wall heading for the way he had come.

He looked closer.

"Bloody cockroaches," he cursed out loud.

He had some stuff that would kill the fuckers in his van he turned to go back and stopped, he could feel things tugging on his boots. He shone his light down and gasped, the cockroaches were trying to bite into his boots, he could feel their tiny jaws on the leather, he shook his feet, but the roaches held fast.

He took a step forward and crunched down on a mass of cockroaches the sound made him sick to his stomach, they were coming at him from all sides now. He tried to run but got a foot caught on something, and then slipped on the carpet of roaches, he fell down and the roaches covered his body. He screamed. A chewing sound could be heard the moaning stopped and then the cockroaches began their journey again; they left the skeleton behind them.

==

Young Tony sighed as he watched a DVD, he looked around his small studio flat, he was an English man working in Spain. He was average height and had brown hair which was cut short, he was of slim build and was a handsome man in his early thirties, and he had been married since he had been twenty-one. The studio had one room for sleeping, he had a pull-out sofa bed, a television in the corner and a cabinet over by the wall, and he had two built in wardrobes with shelves inside, good for storing his stuff. Then he had a small hall which leads to the small kitchen, and off to the left before the kitchen was the small bathroom, which had a toilet a bath and a small sink with an even smaller cabinet over it.

The kitchen had a gas hob which still used gas cylinders and a microwave which Tony used a lot, and a toaster and a kettle. The place was small but ideal for him; he was single and had been since he had split up with his wife four months ago, it still hurt him she had run off with a Spanish man.

All that trouble he had done for her, giving up his job in England, leaving his family and coming to Spain with hers, they had been living with her mum and dad since they got to Spain. He should have known something was wrong when he got an offer to rent a flat, it was a nice place and not far from her mums but no she had turned it down, God if only he had used his brain at the time.

They had talked about getting out for ages then she turns a good place down, and starts acting funny towards him. He would never forget what her family done to him, after all the years they had been married, once the bitch had told him that she wanted some space, oh no she was not seeing anyone she had said. So, he had started looking for a place her family had treated him like shit saying behind his back but making sure he heard it, "why do we have to feed him still."

So, it had carried on and she and her mum would go out to the Chinese and leave him at home, he had never felt so low and like an outcast in all his life. But he had found this place and of course he had known she was seeing someone all along and finally found out from one of his friends.

He remembered the night when he had asked her round his studio to talk, he had been drinking all afternoon and was high on some weed another friend had given him. He couldn't remember much about it in truth, but she said he had said he was going to kill her and she had run out of the flat crying, damn he wished he could remember he would love to see that bitch scared and crying. Tony got up from the sofa and put his plate in the sink, he saw a cockroach on the floor and stamped on it, he lifted his shoe and saw the mess on the floor, "Got you."

He went to bed half hour later, he couldn't be bothered to pull the bed out so just slept on the sofa, and it was comfortable. Unknown to Tony the apartment upstairs were having there's fumigated, the apartments had been besieged lately with a horde of cockroaches; Tony worked all day and didn't know any of this.

==

At first, he didn't know where he was, something had walked across his face, he waved at his face, and was disgusted to feel a cockroach. He slapped it away from him, he was in his studio and had been in a deep sleep and the fucking roach had woken him. He could hear a noise like hard shells rubbing together, it was all over the apartment, he got up and in the semi darkness he could see roaches on the carpet.

He went over to the light and switched it on, the floor was covered in roaches, big fuckers as well they were as big as small rats, small rats with shells on.

But he didn't find this amusing, he went down the hall and into the bathroom, the things were crawling all over his toothpaste and his tooth brush in the glass. A large cockroach climbed over the bar of soap on the side of the bath, he saw that they were coming up from the bath plug hole.

He heard a sound above and looked up and he saw that they were also coming out of the air vent in the wall by the ceiling. He was bare foot and stepped backwards, roaches went over his feet, and he picked up a can of fly spray and aimed it at the roach on the bar of soap.

As he pushed the button, he felt pain in his feet and cried out, the spray hit the roach and made the thing stop for a second, he dropped the can of fly spray and looked at his feet; blood was coming out of tiny wounds on his feet. He kicked out, but they stuck to his feet, he ran into the main room, roaches moved up his legs and he cried out as they bit into his flesh, blood ran down his legs. He stood there in agony and looked at his studio, it was covered in roaches, he had nowhere to run, and they began to fall from the ceiling attaching themselves to his face and head.

==

Clive and Denise had been married for eight years, he was ten years older than her, and he had a round happy face and just a small amount of hair left which went round the sides of his head leaving the middle bald. He was fifty-three and loved his wife even if things were strained sometimes what with working in a bar, well not working owning the bar and working.

She was a pump woman with sandy hair which was cut short and made her look like in truth a Lesbos, but no one ever told her that. She was a happy woman and they both knew Tony from below, he worked for a drinks company and delivered drinks to their bar and also at weekends he would drink and chat with them in their bar. Now living with Clive and Denise was Clive's mother Maureen, she was nearly eighty and looked good for it.

She dyed her hair blonde but it suited her and she had a sweet smile, and was in very good health for a woman her age. They lived above Tony in one of the bigger apartments; theirs had two bedrooms a big kitchen and living room and a much bigger bathroom and toilet. Clive sat in front of the television it had been a quiet day at the bar, well it was a Tuesday, it only really picked up at the weekends, and even then, sometimes that wasn't that good.

He heard a scream from down below, that was Tony but it was muffled and could have been a cry of joy, maybe young Tony had a woman down there, good on him. He remembered the time Tony had been so pissed at their bar they had to carry him home, then he had broken his key in the lock and started to kick at his door screaming and cursing at it.

They had dragged him away and let him sleep on the sofa the next day they had called a locksmith and it was found that if Tony had put the broken key in which had fallen down by the door and turned it in the lock the door would have still opened, Clive had to laugh. Denise was dying herself down after her bath, Maureen had complained that she was not feeling too good and had gone to bed.

Denise would look in on her, she could hear a noise like shells rubbing together and it seemed to be getting louder. She opened the bathroom door and saw two cockroaches run across the hall carpet; they had come from Maureen's room. Denise went up to the door the towel wrapped around her pump body, she opened the door, the noise was louder in there, and she stepped into the room and saw something moving on the bed.

She switched on the light and stood there in horror, the bed was alive with cockroaches and the moving mass was Maureen's body, she felt tiny pin pricks on her feet and cried out. The cockroaches moved to her en mass, she saw the skeleton on the bed and put her hand to her mouth, the cockroaches swarmed over Denise.

Clive heard the loud sound coming from the hall and then he heard his wife cry out, he got to his feet and saw five or six large cockroaches on the floor. Of course, it wasn't unusual to see cockroaches they saw those most days, but these were bigger. He moved into the hallway and saw more cockroaches coming out of his mother's room, he stepped on them hearing them crunch underfoot. But it was too much for poor Clive the sight of the skeleton on the bed, and his wife's body covered in cockroaches, he let out a scream as he felt bites on his ankles and legs, he ran.

He raced down the short hallway across the living room which was filling up with roaches, and opened the double glass doors which lead to the balcony. He stepped onto the balcony the pain in his legs making him winch, he looked back one last time and saw the horde of roaches he grabbed the rail around the balcony and jumped over the top. There was a sickening thudding sound and for Clive the terror was all over.

==

Why hadn't anyone noticed the damn cones flashing all day yesterday, Police chief Ramos looked at the apartment block in front of him?

They had sent down a policeman in the drain and when he came up, he was as white as a ghost telling them of a skeleton wearing drainage overalls, it had started out as a bad day and would probably finish as one. There was a swimming pool to his left not a bad sized one either, palm trees surrounded the pool and they had done a good job, it looked a nice area. Then there was the blanket over the place where the body had fallen from the top floor, the calls had been coming into the station since last night.

Angry residents surrounded the apartments scared to go inside, his men were trying to calm them down, as far as they could tell around ten people had been killed in the apartments by of all thing's killer cockroaches.

Of course, Ramos had scoffed at such an idea but now he had seen the worried people and had seen the dead body which had fallen from the balcony it had been half eaten. He could still see the man's half eaten face starring up at him the teeth shining through the holes in his cheeks.

The pest inspectors arrived ten minutes later, no one was allowed into the building not even the police, food and coffee were brought in for the residents who refused to move away and the policemen. Ramos drank his coffee as he watched the pest inspectors go into the building, their little back packs made of metal shining in the morning sun, and they were going to spray the whole blood place.

==

Ramos drank his coffee and then he felt a tap on his back he turned round and saw a small man before him, Ramos was a big lump of a man six three and a beer belly to match. The short man smiled at him and said, "I'm Alex from the centre for pest control."

Ramos shook hands, "Police Chief Ramos."

Ramos rubbed his big bush beard and looked at the little man. He was clean shaved and had brown hair and thick glasses, and the guy was probably as blind as a bat.

"So, what can you tell me Alex?"

Alex sighed, "Its not good news Ramos."

"So, tell it's been a bad day so far anyway."

"I looked at the roaches and found that they have mutated not only bigger, but they inject a fluid into the skin and this allows them to feed on the flesh of humans. It sort of softens the skin and makes it smell of a substance that the roaches can't resist."

"Great so we have man eating cockroaches."

"I'm afraid so chief."

'Tell me how we can kill the damn things please."

"That's the good news there is a way to kill them."

"So don't keep it to yourself Alex."

Ramos found himself quite liking the scientist; he always had an amusing look on his smooth face.

"We have to burn them it's the only way."

"What about the spraying Alex will that kill them."

Alex shook his head.

"No, it will slow them down for a while but that's all."

"Okay thanks Alex lets burn these fuckers."

Ramos walked up to the front of the building and spoke to the pest control boss, he looked worried and then began talking on the two-way radios, it was time to get his men out.

==

Seven men came out of the building, they came over to the boss and Ramos went over.

"Is that all of your men out."

The boss shook his head, he was about sixty and had white hair and a beard, and he looked like Father Christmas.

"No chief we still have two left inside."

"Well bloody get them out I want this place soaked in petrol."

Ramos went off to instruct his men, he wanted drums of petrol now, and he wanted this damn place soaked in the stuff.

Danny looked down the corridor of the apartment block, bloody cockroaches he hated them, and he was from Scotland and had worked for pest control for four years. He loved his own country but after his parents were killed, he felt like a change, and so had moved to Spain. He had three years of doing nothing then the money had started to run out, lucky for him he knew the boss at the pest centre and bingo he had landed himself a job. There was a door open on his left, he went into the flat, it seemed to be clear, he walked into the living room, his radio started to crackle.

He was reaching for the radio when he saw the cockroach, it was just by the sofa, and he saw that the double glass doors were open leading to the balcony this must be where that bloke had jumped. He looked back at the roach now there were a few of them.

"Quick fuckers," he said as he sprayed them, the liquid went over their bodies and he laughed.

He heard a sound like hard shells rubbing together it was loud and it was coming from one of the rooms in the hallway. He walked over to the door and listened, his radio went again, and he would answer the damn thing in a moment. He opened the door and screamed, the room was a sea of black, he could see no walls no furniture nothing but black, the black wave hit him full on and Danny went down under the sea of cockroaches.

Manuel walked into the apartment right on the top, it was away from the other apartments as if it had been built later, it looked like a janitor's quarters, someone who worked there. The apartment was small and he saw pictures of naked women on the walls, porn books on the side board, real hard core porn books, Manuel picked one up and looked at it, damn he thought. He saw videos all sex tapes, the guy was a pervert, he checked the kitchen all clear then went into the bedroom, the skeleton lay on the bed, white pajamas still attached to its bones. Well, he had found the pervert anyway, the fucker probably deserved it, and he turned round and could hear a sound coming from the small hallway.

He walked down holding the nozzle tightly in his hand, he kicked the door open with his boot, it was the bathroom and it was covered in cockroaches, the sound of their hard shells rubbing against each other. Some of the roaches ran up his legs he started to spray the fuckers, but there were so many, he turned and screamed as they bit into his flesh.

He ran into the living room then out of the front door, the nozzle now forgotten as roaches climbed all over his body. They were on his face and he tried to pull them off, but they were stuck fast. He ran over to the edge of the building and fell off the top; he screamed all the way down and then was silent as his body hit the cement slab walk way below.

==

Ramos heard the first scream and then someone shouted that a man was on the top of the building, he moved back and then saw the man jump, he crashed down onto the cement slabs surrounding the apartments. He raced over with two of the pest controls people, the man was dead of that there was no doubt and he was covered in cockroaches, blood oozed out from his body and began to make a thick pool around him.

"Spray him now for fuck's sake," Ramos shouted.

The men sprang into action and began to spray the dead man, the cockroaches tired to run, but were caught in the double spray, and they slowed down and became lifeless, but not dead. The drums of petrol had arrived on the back of a small lorry the police men were unloading them. Ramos went over and began to bark out orders.

"Okay I want the lower floors of this place drowned in petrol understand."

He took a breath and carried on, "I want some of you to pour the petrol into the empty bottles," case loads of bottles were on the lorry as well, it was a thought he had when he had ordered the petrol.

The men set off with the drums, and Ramos went to get another coffee.

The bottom floor was flooded and then the place was set alight, the petrol in the bottles were thrown high into the apartments by the policemen. Ramos ordered the sewer where the skeleton was found to be soaked as well. That was set alight also and Ramos stood back, and watched as the apartment building burned the whole place was now alight and it was some sight, smoke poured into the sky.

"That's the end of it Alex."

Alex had strolled up to the police chief, "I hope so Ramos."

"Don't worry Alex I'm sure we got them all."

"Like I said I hope so."

Ramos laughed and patted the smaller man on the back, yes, he liked his man very much, "I'm off duty now Alex lets go get a drink."

The cockroaches fled the scene en mass, unknown to the men around the building there was an old sewer out let that had been forgotten about for many years, this ran from the apartment block and away to God knew where. The cockroaches swarmed down the old sewer as the building behind them burnt to the ground. (2013)

The end

EIGHT

Through the eyes of the beast

The man walked onto the loose shale, his footsteps sure as he walked on, Darren Evans was in India and not so much as a holiday as an expedition to see if big foot or the yeti existed, it had been his boyhood dream to find evidence of the creature. Darren was five foot nine inches tall and he was a handsome man at twenty-nine with his sandy long hair tied back in a pony tail, and his trim body kept in shape with regular trips to the gym.

He was on the Himalayas the Indian side before you got to Nepal. He had two helpers with him, one could speak English which he was very grateful for, and they had claimed to know caves were the beast lived so he had hired the pair of them. Koppel was the one who could speak English, he was taller than Darren by a good two inches and as thin as a rake as was the other one who was a lot shorter, and whose name was rakish.

"Not far now boss," Koppel said he was just a little way in front.

"You are sure about these caves," It had been a tiring day and Darren was getting a bit pissed off they had been walking for three days now. He adjusted his rucksack on his back and carried on, Rakish bringing up the rear; he had eyes like a hawk and seemed to watch everything. Finally, over a small hill and

Darren saw the caves, there were three all in a row, the middle one was the biggest by far, he hurried down the slope following Koppel.

They reached the three caves.

"What one does the beast live in?"

Koppel seemed very nervous now they had reached the caves.

"It's not wise to go in alone without some kind of weapon boss."

"Alone I'm not going in alone."

Koppel nodded his head sadly at his boss, "Sorry boss we cannot enter the caves it would be against our religion."

Rakish came up behind Darren and tapped him on the shoulder. Darren tuned and the little man grunted something and pushed a thick stick into his hands.

"Rakish says this is a fine weapon he wants you to have it."

'Tell him thank you."

Darren took off his rucksack, "You look after this I will go into the caves."

He headed for the middle one the biggest.

"No boss it's the one on the left-hand side."

He looked at the smaller cave and shrugged and headed towards that one, he paused at the entrance there was a funny smell coming from the cave. It smelt like someone hadn't bathed for a year and also the smell of rotting flesh, Darren gritted his teeth and walked in to the cave, he turned on his flashlight. He swung the flashlight around the cave, the first hollow was small and he had to bend over, he saw a tunnel up ahead and went into that. He could straighten up in the tunnel, and he came out into a larger hollow and stopped dead.

He could see a shape over by the far corner, he moved closer and shone his light at the shape, it looked human but its hair was so long almost to the floor, and he could see long sharp nails, the thing looked at him and he froze. It was a boy or a young man, he had wickedly sharp teeth which he showed to Darren, how long had his boy lived like this it must have been years.

His blue eyes shone in the light, its skin was white and maybe that was because it never went outside much. Then the thing jumped up and ran towards Darren before he could do anything the thing had bitten him on the hand, he cursed out loud.

"Fucker."

The thing ran off and Darren saw another tunnel, his hand was bleeding badly, and he didn't want to follow the boy thing. He went out the way he had come and saw the two helpers smile with relief as he came out, and then they saw his hand. Koppel put his hand to his knife in his belt.

"You did not get bitten please say."

Darren was all of a sudden scarred the look on his helper's face was one of sheer terror.

"If you were bitten its very bad boss," he gripped the knife handle.

Darren made up something on the spot, "No don't worry I slipped inside and fell on some jagged rocks."

Luckily, they saw the hand and the skin was torn off it could easily have been sharp rocks, they didn't look too hard and Darren bandaged up his wound.

"I saw something in the cave it looked like a boy."

Koppel nodded his head, "That would be the beast then."

"But I'm looking for the yeti Koppel not a boy with long hair and nails."

"That is the beast boss."

That was the end of the discussion, and Koppel made his way back, they followed him.

==

On the second day on their journey back they decided to camp in a snowy rocky area, the rocks would protect them from any high winds in the night. Darren got his tent out from his rucksack, his two helpers just had what looked like animal hides which they lay on. Darren went into his tent without saying good night the

Indians didn't seem to think it necessary to say such things, "What was good about the night," Koppel and told him once.

Darren took off his bandage and gasped, the wound on his hand had healed, there was a tiny red mark and that was all. He looked at his hand in amazement, he had felt no pain in the last two days, but it had grown cold and he thought it was because of that. The full moon rose in the night sky and Darren could see the round shape through his tent. He had a pain in his chest and then it went over all of his body, his body was on fire and he screamed. His clothes were irritating his skin and he quickly ripped them off.

Koppel got his knife from his belt and held it out in front of him; Rakish sat up on his animal hide and watched. Koppel should have known that the beast had bitten him, but he had so wanted to believe the white man, he was a good man and the Indian felt this. He moved closer to the tent the screaming had stopped and now there was a heavy breathing coming from inside. The flaps of the tent were zipped up then as Koppel leaned closer a clawed hand ripped out of the tent; it had sandy hair its arm and hand.

The hand easily ripped the tent open and stepped onto the snow-covered ground, Koppel dropped the knife and starred in horror at the beast before him, the beast stood on its two legs, its huge chest rising and falling. The long snout sniffing the air its dark green eyes fixed on the cowering Indian before it. The sandy colored beast ripped the Indians stomach open with one mighty swing of its arm.

The Indian started to cough up blood as he tried in vain to hold his insides in, his intestines slipped through his fingers and fell steaming onto the cold snow. The Indian fell on his knees and then fell face first into the snow, blood started to pour out of his opened stomach, and the beast got onto its knees and started to feed on the intestines, pushing them hungrily into its mouth.

Rakish cried out and moved away from the scene had the beast heard him he didn't think so, he raced into the rocks and hid behind a large one. The night was a cold one and Rakish shivered, it was maybe half a day to his village, if he started now, he would be there by day break. He heard rocks falling down to his right and looked wildly about he could see nothing in the dark, he moved around the large rock and walked into the beast.

He cried out and prayed to his gods to save him the beast took off his head with one swipe of its hand. Rakish body stood for a moment hand's clenching and unclenching blood pumping out of his stump then fell in a heap on the rocky ground, the head rolled and stopped on the snow-covered ground just past the rocky area.

Darren awoke the next morning he was not in his tent in fact he was not be the camp site at all, he looked around and saw the village close by. He was naked and freezing, he remembered the dream god it had been so real. He stood up and walked into the village a young girl saw him first and ran inside, a man came out and saw the white man who had hired his brother Rakish.

==

They found someone who could speak English after Darren had been escorted back to his hotel room; he was glad to be in the warmth, his room had an open fire, and the landlord and made the fire for him with extra wood to keep it going. He was so cold it took him a while to warm his body, he looked around the single room, there was a bed surprisingly comfy and a small chest of draws for his clothes, a sink and a toilet and bathroom was down the hallway.

It was cheap and the only place in the village you could stay, Rakish brother had come back with the English-speaking man now Darren felt strong again in fact he felt extremely strong like he could rip a man in two with his bare hands. They sat down by the fire in his room, the English-speaking man was called Jacob a Christian Indian and he was small and old, and had white hair and a white beard which was so bushy you could keep birds' nests in there.

"Rupesh wants to know about his brother Rakish.'

Darren nodded his head he had made up a story while he had been warming himself up.

"The two men had an urgent job and they left me near the village after we failed to find anything in the caves on the mountain. I was robbed of all my clothes and rucksack by three thieves' and left to die in the cold."

These were simple people and they seemed to believe me.

Jacob spoke again after talking with Rupesh.

"Okay Rupesh believes you how long will you stay in the village."

"After tonight I am going back to Latur."

The man nodded his head and told Rupesh who kept looking at the white man.

"Fine he hopes you will have a safe trip and he hopes to see his brother soon."

Darren had fallen asleep and slept well into the evening, he awoke suddenly on the bed his body was burning up he saw the embers of the fire, and then everything went blank.

The young girl sneaked out of the hut and quickly walked behind the group of huts, she was a simple girl like all the villagers and she was going to see her love. It was forbidden to see the opposite sex until you married in this village, her father would kill her if he found out, but she didn't care. She was in love with his man and didn't want to marry the man her family had chosen for her he was fat and horrible. She went into a group of trees and to their favorite spot, he was waiting for her and she could see his teeth as he smiled in the darkness.

She had seen the white man's penis this morning as he had walked naked into the village, it had been big even when it was limp, it was much bigger than the man's she loved, but she didn't mind that. She kissed him and felt between his legs and she could feel that he was hard; she was a very sexual girl and needed to have sex.

She had sex with her lover five times now, and she enjoyed it so much and the thought of having sex with the horrible fat man repulsed her. She heard a sound; it was like deep breathing and it was coming from just in front of her and behind her lovers back. Her lover jerked forwards and she stepped back, in the light from the full moon she saw something sticking out of his chest and she let out a scream when she realized it was a clawed hand. It had ripped through her lover's chest from behind, blood poured out of her lover's mouth, and his body hit the ground.

The beast was upon her in a flash, she felt pain in her cheek as it lashed out at her in frenzy. It tore her arm off and blood sprayed over the trunks of the trees, she felt the beast biting into her throat and the world went black. The beast finished its meal and walked out of the trees it looked up at the full moon, and let out a howl.

==

That had been two weeks ago, the dream had bothered him for a few days it had been so real, as he left the village the men folk were looking for a young girl and boy, he left before he heard if they found them. He would see a doctor if these nightmares continued, but when he got back to Latur he found he slept very well, and his girlfriend Lynne had been so pleased to have him back, she was not interested in searching for big foot.

They had rented a villa for two months; it was ideal now they had two weeks left to enjoy India before going back to England and his boring job as an accountant. He had told Lynne about his adventure in the Himalayas, and the two helpers who had gone missing and left him for dead, then the village and the missing girl and boy, and of the villagers talk that the beast had returned from the caves.

Darren felt tense this day, he and Lynne had gone shopping there was a supermarket close by and you could get frankfurter sausages there which helped in this place you could hardly get anything worth having apart from chicken and buffalo beef.

But it was nice to have a treat from chicken and beef curries and have sausages and sometimes chicken nuggets. Darren sat on the chair and closed his eyes god he was bored. The full moon rose in the sky as Lynne woke him up, he was covered in sweat.

"Darren what's wrong honey."

She was a tiny woman and thin, next to Darren she was a dwarf, she brushed his hair back from his head his pony tail had come loose. He starred at her and cried out in pain.

"My body is burning."

She quickly ran into the bathroom, she had some tablets that helped if you got the fever, she found the bottle and went back into the living room the chair was empty and Darren's clothes were scattered about the room.

"Darren honey I got some pills," she said weakly holding up the pill bottle.

The beast attacked her from behind, it tore her back open as it sliced through her clothes and skin with its sharp claws, she screamed once and then fell dead to the floor the beast kneeled down, and began to eat.

==

The policeman heard the howling and stopped, there were monkeys in the fields around Latur, but he had never heard of any wolfs roaming about. He walked on down the dirty street; most people had gone to bed by now, a lot of the villagers just slept by the road with blankets or in empty carts. He saw an old crone sleeping in a door way, the door way was crumbling and old as her, she had no teeth as she snored with her mouth open. He carried on he hated working the night shift he would rather work the day and get the bribes. He was an expert on getting money out of the scooty cab drivers most of them didn't have a license, and for a few rupees he would let them go it was a good scam.

He walked on and kicked a rock, he heard a scooty cab going past he could have waved it down, but thought what the hell. He heard a noise over to his left between two old buildings that looked as if they had seen better days, like most of the buildings in latur.

He took out his hand gun and walked into the dark recess between the two buildings at first, he thought it was a stray dog panting, but then he saw that the thing in the darkness was standing on its two feet like a man. He screamed as the beast took him it smashed him across the mouth ripping open his cheek, and then lifted him off the ground as if he were a toy doll. He was hit against the building so hard that the building shuddered. The beast ate noisily and when it had finished it looked up at the full moon and howled.

The dream had been so real damn he thought they had left him for good, he saw that he lay naked on the bed and alone, Lynne must be up and about. He had dreamed of killing her he felt so bad about that, and then the policeman it had been like looking through the eyes of the killer. Maybe he was ill that's all it was, he got up from the bed and rubbed his face, but he felt so good he had to admit like an athlete. He went into the bathroom and stepped into the shower and turned on the water they only had cold water here, but that was fine the days were so hot who the hell needed hot water.

"Lynne darling are you okay," he called out.

He dried himself and thought maybe she went out; he went back into the bedroom and dressed. He walked into the living room and stopped he saw all the blood it seemed to cover the whole room. It was up the sides of the walls all over the floor, and he saw the half-eaten remains of his girlfriend, and the dreams all flooded back to him. He looked at his hands and saw the red mark where he had been bitten by the boy in the caves.

"That is the beast," Koppel had said and he was right.

He began to sob into the room looking at his hands and saying.

"It can't be me." (2013)

The end

Nine

Zombie patrol

(Outside the safe zone)

The two men were silent for a moment as the patrol car mounted a small hill and came down the other side. They were patrol cops, and were on a mission as always to kill as many zombies as possible in three days and then return to the safe zone. The only safe place left was called the safe zone a place inhabited by survivors of the zombie virus, and now they were a load of television game show junkies. There was a prison zone where all the dangerous men were kept, why they didn't feed them to the zombies was because they used the prisoners as game show contestants. The new show filmed at the game zone island called zombie zone was a great success, the people loved it.

The contestants had to go through jungle terrain and battle certain tests like a horde of zombies under a bridge that looks like it will collapse, and battle for three days until they reach the golden temple then the first one inside and to open the door wins freedom into the safe zone.

Mark West had his feet up on the dash board as he watched the country side around him he was thirty-two and had light brown hair and a goatee. He was a handsome man and well built a testament to the long hours in the gym, he loved being a safe zone cop, but hated these zombie patrols it was bloody dangerous, but the safe zone wanted the zombies dead all of them even if it took a hundred years.

Sydney Wright was the opposite he was a fat slob of a man but had a great sense of humor and that's why Mark liked him so much, Sydney was fifty-three and had a bald head and a round chubby face. He too loved being a safe zone cop, but again hated these damn zombie patrols, but everyone on the force had to do them in a shift rotation bases.

"Hey Mark did I tell you about the time I worked in my sister's beauty shop only lasted a day but as funny as fuck."

Mark went into deep thought Sydney had told him so many stories over the years.

"I don't think so mate," he replied.

"I was young about eighteen I think and she wanted help for the day so I was doing nothing and said OKAY sis."

He paused as he drove round an abandoned car on the road, they were going through the countryside heading towards the city, cities were bad places, and you didn't want to stay in them to long.

"Any way this woman is lying down, and she has those things on her eyes."

"Cucumbers," Mark put in for him.

"Yes, that's the things and my sister has to go answer the phone so I'm left there on my own, well this woman she was nice man, I mean."

Sydney put his hand to his chest to show Mark that she had large breasts.

"And all of a sudden she says to me give me a facial."

Now Mark knew where this was going, but he kept quiet.

"I was young the only facial I knew was from watching porn films, so I whipped out my hard cock and wanked a load of cum all over her face and mouth. I saw her swallow some and that made me cum even more, her face was covered mate."

He laughed and went on, "She screamed the fucking place down I can tell you and in comes my sister and sees me with my cock in my hand, and her friend with a face full of cum."

"Fuck off Sydney that's bull shit man."

"I swear on my life its true mate I never lived it down I was lucky the girl calmed down and saw the funny side I could have gone away for that."

"Oh, come on that's crap no one would do that."

"I swear on my not getting bitten by a zombie it's true."

"We are all going to get bitten by zombies at some time mate."

"Yes maybe."

"If we keep going on these bloody zombie patrols we will."

Sydney nodded his head in agreement, "Damn right mate."

==

They drove on into the night along the small country lanes.

"You see the zombie zone last week," Sydney asked his mate.

"Yes, it was rigged mate no one was going to win that one."

"I think you are right but it was good fun to watch, I liked it when they had the zombies swing down from trees on those elastic ropes" and he let out a laugh.

'I thought it was good when the last two reached the golden temple and that bloke shots the cunt and runs off to win the contest himself."

"Yes, that was a good bit, but then the last door contained zombies the fucker didn't stand a chance."

Mark nudged Sydney with his elbow.

"Hey mate what's that," and he pointed to a small cottage not too far away the lights were on. Of course, everyone in the safe zone had heard stories of survivors living outside the safe zone, but very few had been exactly seen by anyone.

"Hey man could be people," Mark said to him.

"What real people out here no way."

"Then why are the lights on."

"Let's go take a look and see shall we."

Sydney turned the car onto the dirt path that led up to the cottage, the car was a ford and had metal wire over all windows and big head guards on the front and back.

The two men carried pump action shot guns and walked slowly up to the cottage front door, they had seen no movement around them, Sydney knocked on the front door and they waited. The door opened and a man stood before them, he quickly ushered them in side and locked the door, he leaned against the door and sighed. He was a small man a lot shorter than the two cops and he wore glasses, and had a pony tail he looked like a lecturer in a college.

"Thank god you found me I have had the lights on every night for an hour hoping someone would see them."

He had a whiny voice and Mark didn't like him at once, he looked at Sydney and could tell he thought the same thing; there was something wrong about all this.

"Are you alone mister," Mark held up his gun.

"Hey no need for the guns guys."

"Are you alone," Mark hissed at him once more.

"My name is Keith and I'm so glad you found me."

"Keith is there anyone else in the cottage," this time it was Sydney who spoke.

The man paused and seemed to ponder the question; he looked from one to the other.

"Hey men tell me your names."

"I'm Sydney and this is Mark now are you alone."

He held out his hand, "It's been so long since I spoke to real people Mark and Sydney."

Mark put his gun up and aimed at the man's chest, "Stay there Keith."

The man put his hand down, "No need to be like that guys."

"Okay Keith, we will take you back to the safe zone," Sydney said the man had to be alone.

"What about my wife and kids."

"I asked you before were you alone dick head," Mark said gritting his teeth.

'You didn't give me a chance to answer my wife and kids will have to come with us."

"Where are they," Sydney asked.

"I will show you come," the man set off down the short hallway they passed the living room on the left it was dirty and unclean like it hadn't been cleaned in years spider webs covered most of the furniture.

"How long you been here Keith."

Keith smiled at Sydney and replied, "Forever."

He opened the door and the smell hit them, it was so over powering that Mark began to gag, Sydney pushed the man up against the wall and had the gun barrel on his throat.

"What the fuck is in there," he shouted at the man.

"Go and see," he whined at them.

Mark had a handkerchief to his nose and mouth and went inside it was a bedroom, the light switch didn't work so he used his flash light. He moved it around the dark room and stopped, on one bed there was a naked woman tied down. She was rotten and struggled to get out of her bonds, her green like skin was repulsive, and foam came out of her ruined mouth.

He heard another sound and moved the flash light farther round the room, inside a wire cage were two zombie kids, they gripped the bars and growled at Mark, he was feeling really sick but held it down. He went out of the room.

"The sick fucker had his wife and kids locked up they are fucking zombie's man."

'They are my wife and kids you cunt."

"Its sick man his wife is naked and tied to a bed, and the kids are in some kind of cage.'

"Is this true fucker," Sydney's voice went hard.

"Cover this piece of shit I will deal with this," Sydney said to Mark who nodded that was fine with him. Sydney went into the bedroom and using his flash light saw the dead wife, he shot her in the head her head exploded like a water melon, bits of brain and gore covered the wall behind. He took out his hand gun and shot both zombie kids in the head first the little girl, and then the boy.

"No," the man shouted after the first shot, but Mark kept the gun on him, then two more shots and the man began to cry.

"You killed my wife and kids they were all I had left."

Sydney walked out of the room his face a fury of temper; he pushed Mark out of the way and shot the man against the wall with the shot gun to the chest. He let out a moan and slid down the wall leaving a long smear of blood behind him.

"Let's get the fuck out of here," Sydney said.

Mark spat on the dead man and said, "Damn right fucking freak."

==

They drove in silence for a while it was getting late now.

"That was some weird shit man," Mark said.

Sydney nodded "Yes it was, the man was insane we had no choice but to shot him."

"Damn right we can't take loonies back into the safe zone."

Mark was silent for a minute and then said to his mate, "Do you think he was fucking his wife I mean she was naked and tied down well?"

Sydney thought about this and replied, "You know what I think he was the sick fuck."

Mark let out a yawn, "Let's find a place to park up and sleep Sydney.'

Sydney nodded his head he was feeling sleepy too.

He drove on and then spotted a clump of trees, he pulled over and drove into the trees, and it was as good a spot as any.

"Did I tell you about the time I was window cleaning with my mate?"

Mark smiled one more story before bed, "No I don't think so."

"We had this window cleaning round in the day, we done well and there was this one old couple really nice people always gave us tea and biscuits."

He coughed a little and went on, "One day we are there drinking our tea in the conservatory any way for a laugh I start touching his hand and calling him darling, and telling him I love him."

He let out a laugh and Mark couldn't help laughing with him, "We didn't hear them but the two old people were right behind us and when we looked round, they had this sort of horrified look on their faces needless to say we didn't clean their windows again, but boy it was funny just to see the look on their faces."

He let out a huge belly laugh and Mark joined in, "I would have loved to see that," he laughed.

The two men relaxed and rested back in their seats.

"Good night, Sydney."

"Good night, Mark sleep tight."

"Hey Mark do you know where that came from."

"What."

"Sleep tight."

"No go on quickly tell me."

"William Shakespeare courted his lady to be Anne Hathaway in this cottage called Anne Hathaway cottage any way the straw mattress of the finely carved oak Hathaway bed was held up by a network of ropes which had to be tightened hence the saying night, night, sleep tight."

"No bullshit Sydney."

"No bullshit mate."

"That's real interesting night mate."

"Night night sleep tight," giggled Sydney to his friend.

Mark had a bad dream he couldn't remember what it had been about but a bad dream meant a bad day that's what his mother had always said to him. The first thing he saw when he looked out of the window screen was the ruined face of a zombie, the man zombie had one eye missing and the left side of his face was burnt, it was trying to bite the wire mesh over the window.

"Holy fuck," Mark shouted out.

Sydney awoke and looked in shock at the burnt zombie on the window screen.

'What the fuck.'

They both looked at each other and then out at the early morning light, there were about ten zombies roughly around the car. Some tried to pull the wire mesh off with their hand's others tried to bite it, there was a nurse wearing her uniform she was wandering about the bushes. Mark saw an army man wearing his uniform he had a massive wound down the side of his face, and one of his hands was missing he was banging on the back window with his stump. Sydney started the car.

"Okay we drive off and park up ahead and then start shooting the fuckers okay."

"Sounds good to me mate."

Sydney may have been still sleepy that's why he did what he did, he stepped on the accelerator the hand brake was off and the car shot forwards, and smashed head first into a tree. Mark hit his head on the window screen, Sydney cried out and managed to put his hands up to stop himself flying forwards, but in doing so broke both his wrist's, he cried out in agony. The car's bonnet was smoking and the smoke was covering everything, they were still safe inside for the moment. Mark groaned and put his hand to his forehead, he was bleeding but it wasn't too bad, damn what the hell had happened. He heard his good friend sobbing besides him.

"What's up mate are you okay?"

"It's my wrist's they are both broken," he hissed out between clenched teeth.

"We need to get out of here mate find another car and head back."

Sydney nodded his head, "Okay let's move you are going to have to be my gun."

Mark then realized his mate couldn't shot. He opened his door and got out smoke was everywhere, he couldn't see the zombies and went round to his mate's side, he opened the door and helped him out a zombie grabbed his arm. Mark yelled out and let go of his mate, he brought up the shot gun and blew the zombies head off, blood covered his own face and he spat out some, shit did that mean he was infected, he wasn't sure but someone had said don't swallow the infected blood. Had he swallowed some he wasn't sure he could taste it in his mouth alright. He saw the nurse zombie and shot her in the stomach.

"The head you wanker," Sydney shouted he was moving away from the car and the smoke, and heading for a field.

Mark lifted up the gun and shot her in the head; the top of her head exploded and left the jaw line intact, she collapsed to the ground. His gun was grabbed by a woman zombie, her shirt was open and she had no bra on, her big tits flopped about as she wrestled with the gun. He kicked her and she went backwards, he shot her in the head. He heard Sydney scream and turned round.

Sydney was in agony as he moved away from the wreaked car, how the fuck had all this happened it was just a simple zombie patrol in and out take no risks, they had fucked up royally. He was heading away from the smoke and could see a field just ahead, his hands were on fire and he thought he might pass out, but he gritted his teeth and went on. Something grabbed him from behind, he reached down instinctively for his hand gun, pain shot up his arm, and he cried out.

The zombie reached forwards and took a large chunk of his flesh from his cheek, blood gushed out of the wound, and Sydney screamed out in pain. He turned and saw the army zombie with the missing hand chewing on his flesh, Mark came from behind and the things head exploded, and blood covered Sydney.

He stood there in shook and then collapsed to the ground out cold. Mark bent down and picked up his buddy's head in his arms, he was crying tears came down his cheeks as he saw the ruined cheek of his friend, it was too late for Sydney now. He turned and saw the rest of the zombies staggering towards him he stood up and took out his hand gun, he aimed and shot his mate in the forehead. He thought about going back to the car for more ammo, but there seemed to be more zombies now coming out of the smoke, he ran into the field.

==

Mark doubled back on himself and headed towards the safe zone, as long as he kept to the quiet country lanes, he was sure he would be okay. He walked quickly on damn he was hungry he had left everything at the car. He was sure he would make the safe zone by tomorrow afternoon he would have to find somewhere to sleep rough, but hell he was used to that shit.

He walked along a country lane and stopped and looked ahead, there was a tunnel which went under the road above, when they had come, they had gone over the tunnel, the inside of the tunnel looked dark. What should he do, he was caught between just climbing up the sides of the road, and it was a high climb or taking a chance in the tunnel?

He took out his flash light what the hell, he could see a car blocking the tunnel entrance looked as if someone had swerved and hit the tunnel sideways blocking it slightly. Mark got up to the car, he held the shot gun tight in one hand and the flash light in the other, he walked round the crashed car and entered the tunnel.

He could see the light coming from the other side it wasn't that far, he moved slowly through the dark tunnel. His leg hit something and he looked down, there was a motor bike on the ground, and petrol ran from its burst fuel tank. He moved on and heard a noise to his right he swung the light round and saw a large rat run off into a hole in the brick wall, his heart was thudding in his chest as he moved on.

Then a hand grabbed his jacket, he wrestled with the thing, but it had his jacket held fast, Mark slipped out of his cop jacket and brought the shot gun round. He held the flash light to the barrel and saw the zombie in front of him the thing was trying to chew his jacket. The zombie looked like some kind of construction worked it had a red lumber jack shirt on, and a yellow hard hat.

He shot the zombie in the head, its face and the hard hat exploded and blood and gore went over his jacket, he would leave that be. He breathed a sigh of relief as he made it to the other side he stood in the light of day, and turned back towards the tunnel, a small zombie girl was coming after him, she must have been no more than five, and she held onto her teddy and dragged it along the ground.

She had a dirty Barbie girl t-shirt her blonde hair covered most of her face thankfully and Mark aimed and blew her head off he tuned quickly he didn't want to see this, and walked away from the tunnel. He walked on up the country lane he came to a car smashed into another car, he saw two dead bodies in one car they must have been dead for a while and were starting to look like skeletons.

Flies buzzed around them; the other car was empty but had loads of blood in the front seat. Now the safe zone was close but he needed to cross the woods that would be safe, the country lanes were giving him the willies all these bends he never knew what to expect when he rounded one, he headed off into the woods instead.

==

As he walked in the woods, he decided that he had done right the shade of the trees was welcoming, the day was a warm day and he was covered in sweat mainly from being shit scared in the tunnel, there was a slight breeze that felt like heaven on his hot body. He was starting to get a fever was it the blood he had swallowed or was he just imaging it all, the day was hot he reasoned.

He came across a small building this side was in the woods, but as he went round to the front, he saw that it was on a road and there was a car park in front of the building maybe he could get some food and water it was worth a quick look. As he came out of the woods, he saw that it was a furniture store he looked in and couldn't see any zombies.

He saw wooden beds on half price and a wooden cabinet with seventy per cent off, the front door was swinging open and closed in the slight breeze. He entered the store and walked down a short hall way on his right he saw a reception desk; he had a quick look, but could see no food that would be in the canteen hopefully.

He turned left and went into the store front he could see no zombies just furniture. He walked past the seventy per cent off cabinet and sat on one of the wooden beds if this place was clean then maybe he could hole up here tonight. Yes, he made up his mind he would check the rest of the place out, and then lock it down tight.

He went back into the hallway and saw a stair way leading up hopefully to the canteen; he went up the stairs holding his shot gun out in front of him. There was an office to the right with a large window looking out at the front of the store this must have been the manager's office. He went in and had a quick look round; he spied a whisky bottle and took it the bottle was half full.

He walked farther there was some kind of conference room, a large room with a wall television and lots of chairs, and then he came to the last door it had to be the canteen and it was closed. There was a smell in the air of rotting corpses was it coming from outside or was it coming from inside he could not tell, he tried the door knob the door was locked.

He stepped back down the hallway and took aim he would blow the door open it didn't matter too much if zombies heard outside, he would soon have this place locked down good for the night. He pulled the trigger and the door exploded in a hail of wooden splinters as the smoke cleared, he saw a horde of zombies rush out of the door way. He saw a fat zombie in the front other zombies were trying to get past him, but he was one big mother fucker he must have been nearly seven foot tall as well as he struggled out the door way Mark took aim, and shot it in the head.

Its head exploded and instead of falling backwards and crushing the zombies behind the fat fucker fell forwards and the other zombies started to climb over its body. Mark stood there for a second damn it was a shame he could have done with a nice bed to sleep on tonight, but the room had been packed with zombies for some reason, maybe someone had rounded them up and put them in the room. Maybe they were here for a conference when the zombie virus hit and they had been pushed into one room who knew all he knew was that he had to get the hell out of here now.

He ran down the stairs taking them two at a time and ran out of the front door and almost slap bang into a zombie woman who was pregnant. He stopped in front of her and looked in horror at the crow bar going through each cheek. The weight of the crow bar made her head slump forward as she walked, the huge bump in her belly just a huge lump of flesh there was no way a baby could survive. He was getting sick of seeing the dead, it was really getting to him now this had meant to be so easy just an in and out job kill as many of the dead fucks as you could, and report back in three days job done.

The pregnant zombie woman reached out to him, he grabbed one end of the crow bar and pushed with all his might the zombie woman toppled over onto her side. He watched as she struggled to get up the weight of the crow bar fighting against her. He walked off into the woods once more, he left the zombie woman on the ground, he was sick of shooting the fuckers.

==

The night closed in on him as he was walking through a group of trees, he didn't want to be on the ground in the woods at night time, you didn't know where the zombies might be. And no doubt those dead fucks he had let out of the canteen room would be spilling into the woods by now as well, he looked up at the trees, he picked a tall strong one and began to climb.

He had used to love tree climbing when he was a boy there had been a dump close to his house, and the kids used it as their playground. He had built their own camp and would sit for hours telling each other ghost stories. There had been black berry bushes and raspberry bushes, but the main thing had been the huge old cherry tree every year it would fruit and they were the best damn cherry's he had ever tasted, and he meant that even now nothing compared to them cherries.

It was good to remember the fun times took his mind off the hell at hand, he climbed onto a thick branch and took off his belt, there was a small branch coming out of the thicker one and he tied himself to this with his belt and lay down. Should he fall in his sleep the belt would hold him, he closed his eyes he was so damned tired.

It was a restless night and he kept waking up and looking down at the ground, he heard noises deep in the woods and owls crying out into the dark, but he managed to sleep in between and finally morning came he was sure he was not far off now. He climbed down the tree and saw a zombie come out of the bushes, he wore a def leopard t-shirt and its jeans were almost round its knees. A young man in life its pure white face frozen in a stare, Mark shot the thing in the head, and walked into the woods.

He decided to walk in the fields it was far too risky walking in the woods a zombie could jump him from behind a tree, the fields were much better, he saw a zombie an old woman probably a farmer's wife, she was wearing an apron her grey hair waving in the breeze. He hit her with the butt of the shot gun and battered her head with the gun until it was just a gory mess, it reminded him of the time he had dropped a bottle of his mother's home-made strawberry jam on the floor.

He walked on he was thirsty and hungry and his stomach kept rumbling as he walked, he was feeling weak, was he infected he still didn't know how long would it take. He had heard stories of up to three days and then as little as two hours each case varied. Then the welcome sight of the safe zone wall, it must have been ten feet tall or more he had never really taken much notice of it before.

He let the shot gun fall to his side as he walked towards the safe zone wall, he must have looked a right state, dried blood on his forehead, dirt all over his clothes and face. As he got closer, he could see guards on the top of the wall shooting at the zombies there was a horde of them close to the safe zone wall. That would have been one of his job's taking it in turns to patrol the wall if you saw any zombies, you were to shoot on sight.

He moved closer to the safe zone wall and was just about to raise his hands above his head and cry out when a bullet hit him square in the middle of his forehead, he fell dead onto his back.

The young cop grinned at his friend that was his first kill; he was new to the job.

"I got the fucker Matt."

Matt smiled at him, "Nice shooting mate." (2013)

The end

Ten

The wolf who dreamed he was a man

The fire roared with life as the old chief put more logs on the fire, seated around the hole where the fire roared was a group of young boys and girls. The village was remote and small, tiny huts littered the surroundings. The small village was way out in the countryside of Latur; they very rarely went into the town only if it was urgent for food or medical supplies. But the village was pretty much self contained, they grew their own food and had a village witch doctor who claimed to cure everything of course he hardly ever got anything right, but thus didn't seem to bother the villagers.

The chief sat down in front of the kids, in the half light from the fire he looked like a demon and some of the kids shuddered, tonight the chief had decided to tell the village kids ghost stories and one in particular. He was a simple man and had thin grey hair and a huge belly that over lapped his groin cloth, but he was a fair and pleasant village chief and he loved all the kids as his own.

One of the little girls looked on in wonder Stuti loved tales of horror; she looked at the chief in awe and sensed that he was going to tell them of a legend, she loved legends because sometimes they were half true. The chief smiled at the kids and began to talk in Hindi to them.

"There is a true legend in these parts about a wolf that wanted to be a man, the wolf often watched the kids playing by the stream of course he could not play with them they would be scared, and run away from him.

He was much more intelligent than the other wolves from his pack, and that's not to say wolfs are not intelligent they are very intelligent animals, but this one was different. One night he howled at the full moon asking the god of man to make him be like the kids playing he felt he was inside the wrong body. Then he had a vision as a white figure came down from the full moon and the god stood before the wolf and granted him his wish.

But he can only be a man on the full moon and must return to being a wolf in the early morning when the moon disappears. Of course, the wolf is delighted and thanked the god of man, his body immediately starts to change, and before not to long he is standing naked before the full moon as a man."

The chief saw that he had all of the kid's attention and went on.

"The legends of werewolf's are said to be made up from this legend of the wolf who dreamed he was a man, but they just changed it round to men changing into wolfs. The wolf soon learnt a great deal about being a man, and had clothes hidden in a tree truck for when he changed at the full moon. He walked amongst men, and even joined in talking with them sometimes and soon he meets and fell in love with a beautiful girl. The girl's name was Stuti."

The chief looked at the tiny beautiful girl sitting by the fire and smiled at her, she seemed to take great pleasure in the fact that he spoke her name.

"Soon after a time the wolf made the girl pregnant and the villagers became enraged as the girl was promised to another. One night a villager saw the young man change back into a wolf and told the rest of the villagers, they hunted down the wolf and after two days they killed the wolf without mercy. They tied its dead body to a tree branch close to the village so everyone could see the dead animal and spit on it. After two weeks they cut down the dead body and burnt it under the tree, a blue smoke came out of the body and the villagers stepped back. The smoke changed into a man and back into a wolf, the villagers fled calling the wolf a demon."

The chief stopped and looked at the kids.

"What happened to the baby," Stuti asked him.

He shrugged his fat shoulders and smiled, "No one knows but it is said that the blue smoke was a sure sign that the wolf would come back again one day to find his beloved Stuti."

==

The wolfs played with their mother on the grass, one wolf stood out from the others he had a brown strip running down his black body, and he seemed more interested in what was going on around him than the others. The mother wolf sensed he was different and tried to keep him in with the other cubs so they wouldn't notice, and maybe push him away from the pack that was one thing she didn't want to happen. But as the years went by the young wolf grew into a fine young male, he would often play on his own.

Chasing the bee's and fly's but he wondered how they could fly, and why were the bees so interested in the flowers, he was always asking questions to himself about everything. He would secretly sneak up to the town border and watch the men, he somehow felt that he was one of them, and would often dream at night that he was in fact a man and not a wolf at all. He dreamed of a woman, a young beautiful woman and he would hold her in his arms and kisses her as a man would. He could even feel the beat of her heart as he kissed her tender lips with his own.

==

Stuti looked at the computer screen it had been many years since her family had lived in the surrounding countryside, her dad had made it big while aboard with his medicine company and when he returned, he had sent for his family, and from then on, they lived in luxury compared to the village, but she never forgot the old chief and the story of the wolf who dreamed he was a man. Stuti was a fine-looking young woman, she had long dark hair and hazel eyes and she was very petite, and moved around with a confident swagger. Along with her tiny body was her tiny little nose and mouth which just added to her beauty she was a catch for any man, and she knew it.

Her father had talked of setting her up with one of his colleague's boys, but she had heard no more about it and hoped it was all forgotten, she wanted to marry the man of her dreams not someone she didn't know. She looked at the computer screen there it was the legend of the wolf who dreamed he was a man, she had found it, she went into the site there wasn't much on the legend, and it soon went onto other legends.

But she read that the wolf changed only on the full moon and had to return at the light of day to the body of a wolf. There was a drawing of the wolf as a wolf and as a man he was very handsome, and his lover Stuti who also got a mention and a drawn picture.

She starred at the picture it could have been her, it was like looking into a mirror, so the old chief had not lied about the name of the girl. She had spent years thinking that he had only said her name to make her feel good, but no it was down with the legend before her on the computer screen. That was it really about the legend, she could not find much else on it, and soon gave up at least she had found a bit about it and she printed off the pages, she would keep these the legend fascinated her.

==

The young wolf looked up at the full moon, he howled at the moon his brothers and sisters came and looked at him, the mother wolf stayed a little way apart looking at her wolf. He had seen men praying at the little temples scattered about the countryside and lighting strange thin poles. He had seen other men walking down the dirty streets of the town and making a sign on their chests, he came to the conclusion that they were praying to different gods. He wasn't sure what a god was, but he howled at the full moon now, howling out to his god and asking to be a man once more, he felt he had already been a man once.

First, he felt a cracking of one of his bones, it was in his leg bone and he looked back, the crack sounded again and his brothers and sisters moved away from him, the mother looking on. His fur started to go inside his skin and soon his body was smooth, he laid on the grass and cried out as his body changed. His legs straightened and grew longer as did his arms, his jaw and mouth and snout sank back inwards, and his smaller nose came out of his face. His eyes went back into his skull and became smaller and hair grew on his bald head, his penis became smaller and hair sprung up around this too, the burning pain in his body stopped.

He sat up and looked at his hands, they were different and he clenched and unclenched them, he laughed at the moon and turned to look at his family. His brothers and sisters walked away from him, and then his mother turned her back on him. They would not attack him, but from his time he was an outcast of the pack. But he didn't have time to be sad he was so excited he ran for the stream and looked into it with his new human face. He looked and saw his sharp features and dark black hair he was much better looking than any man he had ever seen.

He saw his naked body and felt his penis. It was so much smaller than the wolf one, but he suddenly felt it growing hard, that was a bit better he looked at his erection still not as big but not bad. He needed to steal clothes he wanted to go into town and walk among the men and women, and see if they noticed him.

==

He looked at the men's clothes they were hanging over a fence, he crept up to the wooden fence and took the trousers, he tried them on, a little big but otherwise they looked and felt okay, next he took the white shirt and put it on. He didn't have any shoes, but walked into town and soon saw that many men didn't wear shoes so no one noticed in fact no one noticed him at all, he was walking among the men and he was one of them.

He looked at the many faces, some with beards others with mustaches and goatee beards and clean-shaven men, he felt his own face and found it to be smooth, he liked that he had always been covered in fur, and now his body felt free.

He saw the little stalls selling various things to eat and they smelt so good, in fact he could smell food from miles away. His sense of smell had not left him in the change, and his eye sight was as sharp as it had ever been and the muscles under his new skin were tight and stronger, he figured he was much stronger than any man.

A girl smiled at him, he remembered that he was very handsome and smiled back at her, but she carried on past him and was soon gone. How was he meant to get the opposite sex to like him when he was a wolf it was all to do with scents and proving how strong and a good hunter he was.

He was thinking about these things when he bumped into a girl, he didn't see her, he was far too lost in his new thoughts. He looked at the girl without saying anything, she was beautiful and he recognized her somehow, it was the strangest sensation ever, he knew her. He looked the petite girl up and down and at her long flowing dark hair he little nose, and the mouth set in a beautiful oval face, he knew her.

"Excuse me Miss would be nice," she said to him.

He smiled at her and she smiled back at him there was laughter in her eyes.

"I'm sorry Miss," it was the first words he had spoken and he found the words came easy to him.

"That's okay no harm done."

"If I had harmed you, I would never forgive myself."

Now he liked this thing called talking, he had to know more about her.

"What's your name," she asked him.

Name he didn't have a name in the pack he was just a wolf with a scent, he looked wildly about him and his eyes came to rest on a sign.

'My name is Daniel what is your name if you don't mind me asking you."

The sign had read Daniels's bakery and it seemed to be a nice name and rolled off the tongue easy.

"You are a Christian then."

Daniel thought about this and knew it was to do with praying to a god, he didn't know if his god was Christian.

"Yes I am."

"That's good because I am too; we changed from Hindi many years ago."

'Hindi okay," he replied he didn't have a clue what Hindi was but it must be another religion from Christian.

He kept looking at the food stall and she noticed this, she felt like she knew him and felt at ease with him.

"My name is Stuti, and are you hungry Daniel."

It was like an electric shock going through his body as soon as she said the name, he knew her. It was her the girl of his wolf dreams the one he held in his arms the one he kissed with his lips it was Stuti. He smiled at her, "I am very hungry but have no money."

She smiled back at him he was so handsome, "Not to worry about that Daniel come."

He followed her to the stall and she ordered some food, the stall had some old tables and chairs in the dirt, they ate their chow and chili chicken in silence at the old tables. He kept looking at her face and noticed that she returned the look he felt that she liked him too, and she had spent money on him. Her clothes were so much better than his old tatty ones, but she didn't seem to notice, and the fact that he had no shoes didn't seem to bother her. She looked like a queen and he looked like a peasant.

The taste of the food was out of this world, so much better than eating raw meat from the kills as a wolf. The taste of the chow, he could taste the hot peppers and sauce the chilly chicken was spicy, but the cooked chicken was a hundred times better than the raw chicken he was used too. They finished the meal and she stood up, he followed suit and looked into her hazel eyes.

"You have strange eyes for an Indian Daniel."

"Strange," he replied he was getting nervous what was wrong with his eyes, had they not changed properly.

"They are blue that is so rare I have never seen it before, and it is so beautiful."

He sighed and felt himself calming down, she had said his eyes were beautiful.

"Thank you Stuti," her name came off his lips so easily.

"I have to go Daniel, but I would like to meet you again tomorrow."

"Yes, I would like that too Stuti."

"You have a mobile."

He stood there he didn't know what a mobile was, he just shook his head and he saw her looking at his clothes and his bare feet, but she was not judging him.

"No problem lets meet here again and I will buy you food."

"Yes," he felt so wonderful and alive.

"I just want you to know Stuti that I am from a village and we don't have much money and no luxuries just so you know."

She felt so in love with this man before her, she knew him and she knew all about living in a small village.

"That's fine Daniel till tomorrow then."

She took his hand in hers and squeezed it he gently squeezed back, and they smiled at each other before departing. He walked for the rest of the night as men closed up their shops and some people slept on the streets with blankets over them. He saw one in a door way he held out his hand for change and Daniel walked past the old man he had no money to give. He saw clothes shops, beer shops, the smell of alcohol made him feel sick that was one thing he didn't want to try, and a man smoking had breathed into his face. He had a coughing fit for a good few minutes before stopping, the smoke had been awful. So many new things to see and so many different things to do, he couldn't wait to see Stuti tomorrow.

==

Daniel walked back into the woods as the light started to break through the darkness; he knew his time was almost up for this day. He stripped and hid his clothes inside an old tree, there was a hole in the truck of the old tree, he stood there naked not sure what was going to happen to him. As the light got stronger, he lay on the grass and closed his eyes his body began to burn once more, and he cried out in pain as he changed.

He opened his eyes and got to his four paws, he was a wolf once more, and he ran into the woods eager to find his mother and his brothers and sisters. As he drew closer to the pack one of his brothers started to snarl at him and he stopped, his mother turned her back on him once more and walked off, the pack followed.

His brother darted forward and bit Daniel on the leg he cried out in pain, and looped back to a safe distance. He saw the pack disappear they would not kill him, but this was a warning not to find them again, he had lost his wolf family. He was sad but not for long he knew that his future lay in being a human and loving the girl of this wolf dreams, things would turn out fine. He didn't know what was going to happen in his new life and he would have to play it by ear. He only had tomorrow night and then a long wait until the next full moon, but let's live life for the moment he thought, and ran into the woods in the opposite direction to the pack.

==

The pain in his body vanished as he stood once more by the old tree; he took out his clothes and dressed in them. He longed to be with Stuti and his heart raced as he made his way to the food stall, would she be there or would she have just been playing him along and stay at home. As he rounded a bend in the dirty street, he saw the stall and at first couldn't see her then he saw her she was seated by the tables on one of the old chairs. She smiled at him and her eyes went over his body, he could feel his penis getting harder and willed it to go down.

"Daniel you're late," and then she laughed, "Only kidding it's so good to see you."

"I have been waiting all day to be with you Stuti."

She looked at his arm and he saw her face change to one of concern, the wound on his front leg that his brother had caused was bleeding, the blood coming through the white shirt.

"Come Daniel I will get that seen too."

"It's okay Stuti it's just a flesh wound it's nothing."

"Come follow me."

"Where are we going?"

"To my flat of course."

He felt warmness in his belly and his penis was starting to get hard again, going to her home all sorts of things could happen.

She lived alone in a flat her dad had bought her; it was a one bed roomed place with a bathroom and a kitchen plus a small living room, and a wide balcony that she would often sit out in and watch the stars in the night sky. He sat down in the small living room at the table and he took off his shirt, he knew that he had rippling muscles, and he saw her eyes go wide as she looked at his body.

He watched as she put the bandage on his arm after cleaning the wound with salt water and then putting on some disinfectant. There was a strong pull in the room, it was pulling them together they looked at each other, her face went a bright shade of crimson, he held her tiny hand in his and smiled at her.

"I feel I have known you forever Stuti."

She smiled and leaned forwards and kissed him on the mouth. He responded immediately and when they finally broke apart, she took his hand in hers and led him into the bedroom. He took off his clothes and she pointed to the bathroom and smiled, "First a shower."

He nodded at her he could even smell the animal smell on his body.

They made love all that night, he seemed to be able to go on forever and ever, and he made love to her six times before finally falling into a deep sleep. He was surrounded by his brothers and sisters he was in the woods, and he could see the daylight trying to filter through the trees. They were growling and snarling at him, he looked down and saw that he was a man not a wolf, and then one of his brothers spoke.

"You are an outcast and must die as a wolf not a man."

"How can you talk brother?"

"I am no brother to you outcast."

"I want to die as a man if that is what it comes down too."

"Then so be it outcast."

The pack of wolfs dived onto Daniels body, he felt his sister take a chunk out of his arm and he cried out in pain, the brother who had spoken was a big black wolf and took Daniel by the throat, blood poured down Daniels's front and he screamed. He opened his eyes and saw that he was lying on the bed with covers over his body; he looked and saw the daylight. He stood up on all fours he was a wolf, he looked down at Stuti and heard her moan, she was waking up, and he leapt from the bed and saw an open window. Without looking back, he jumped through the window and landed in the dirty street, already people were about and some moved away as they saw him, he raced away from them and headed for the woods.

==

Stuti woke up and saw a flash of color as something leapt out of the far window, she brushed the sleep away from her eyes and got to her feet. She went over to the window and looked down into the dirty street below, again she saw a form racing away in the direction of the woods, was that a wolf, some of the people down below looked shocked, and then returned to what they were doing.

==

He stood before her door the next night, his hand half way to knocking on the door, it had been two weeks since he had leapt out of her window, how was she going to take it, he had a story made up in his mind. He knocked on the front door and waited, it opened slowly and he saw her pretty face looking out at him, there was shock at first and then anger.

"Come on in," she said to him, she shut the door behind her.

"I'm so sorry Stuti but the village needed me, we had a fire and our crops burnt, I had to help plow new fields and plant new crops."

He paused to see if she was buying his story.

"I'm so sorry my love forgive me.'

He bent his head and waited for her reply, she took his face in her hands and kissed him on the mouth, he was amazed he thought that she would not want to see him ever again. He kissed her back and soon they were in bed once more he made love to her passionately, and they were each lost in their love for each other.

Later they walked hand in hand down the dirty streets close to her home.

"I saw a wolf the day you left."

He swallowed hard, "Really,' was all he could say.

He heard a noise from above, part of the old buildings roof was crumbling away. He picked Stuti up in his arms and rushed over to the other side of the street expertly avoiding scooty cars as they went past. He put her down and she looked at him, and then heard the crash as the old buildings roof collapsed just where they had been standing. She looked at the debris, and then back at him.

"How did you know I heard nothing?"

"I have good hearing."

"I need a drink come."

She bought a bottle of whisky and they drank on her balcony, it was his first drink and the smell was bad just like the first time he had smelt it, but once you drank it wasn't so bad and it felt warm going down. She showed him her tiny tattoo, it was on her shoulder.

"Come you must get one done.'

His mind was in a whirl the drink was having an effect on him; he sat in the chair and had Stuti tattooed on his arm. They ended up in her bed again, and he found that he could only make love once and then he felt wasted, he lay down and was soon in a deep sleep.

He was back in the woods and this time he was a wolf standing in front of his brothers and sisters.

"I want to die as a man not a wolf.'

His big black brother looked at him with his evil green eyes.

"You die as a wolf that's how it's meant to be outcast."

Again, he was attacked and he felt the steel jaws clamp on his leg and screamed.

He opened his eyes his brain was still fuzzy he was late again he saw the sun light coming in through the open window. He got up on all fours and stretched his body, and looked down at Stuti. He was looking into her open eyes; she starred at him in wonder then in horror and screamed. He quickly jumped off the bed and ran for the window, he looked back at her and saw that she had composed herself now, she looked at him with a confused face and then he was gone.

He jumped down into the dirty street and raced for the woods, people got out of his way fast, one man tried to kick him and he snarled at the man. He reached the woods what would Stuti do now, she had seen him for what he was a wolf trying to be a man.

==

Stuti got dressed she had to find the wolf she had seen the brown strip along its back it shouldn't be that difficult to find. She now knew that Daniel was the wolf of legend and she was his lover, she had to find him, that's the reason they had known each other. She wasn't sure if she believed in reincarnation, but it looked a strong possibility. She went out the front door it was going to be a long day she had better get water and some snacks if she was going to search the surrounding woods all day. Would he recognize her in his wolf form she was sure he had known who she was when he had jumped out of her window, how would she react when she saw him as a wolf all these questions went round in her mind.

Daniel walked through the woods he was feeling hungry now, he would go rabbit hunting or maybe he would get a mongoose. He enjoyed the chase and the fight with mongoose they were savage little bleeders. He was even thinking like a man in his wolf form that troubled him, why didn't he just return as a wolf, but no he could remember everything and it was like a torture to him, he saw Stuti in his mind's eye always. He trotted along and was not watching where he was going, he was so intent on thinking about everything and trying to figure out why he was a man in a wolf's body.

The bear trap snapped shut on his front leg, the pain shot up his body and he cried out in pain, the steel teeth of the clamp smashed into his bone, he tried to move his leg but pain shot up once more. He let out a howl into the daylight, hoping that someone or something would find him, the pain was intense, he couldn't believe how stupid he had been lost in thought, and not concentrating on where he was going. His mother had shown them traps when they were young, and they knew not to go near them and to look out for them, and now he had done this and he had to see Stuti tonight as a man.

He lifted his head up from the ground he had fallen unconscious; he saw his mother by the side of some trees and his brothers and sisters close by all watching him. He howled out to his mother and with tears in his eyes he saw her trot over to him, she paused before him and he tried to move his injured leg once more, but pain shot through his body and he cried out.

His mother looked him in the eye and bent down to him, she licked him across his face and he could feel the warm moisture of her saliva. She turned her back on him and trotted back into the trees and was gone, his brothers and sisters stood and looked at him for a few seconds, and then they too went back into the woods.

He was losing a lot of blood and he was very weak but tears sprang to his eyes his mother had said good bye to him. He knew he was going to die and now he accepted the fact, he lay his head down and closed his eyes.

==

The young woman pushed yet another tree branch out of her way; she had been in the woods for the better part of the day and not one sighting of any wolves let alone one with a stripe on its back. Her water was almost finished and she had eaten the snacks earlier, she would have to start going back soon. She came into a clearing and saw him up ahead, he was laying with his back to her and she could see the brown stripe, she had found him.

"Daniel," she cried out to him.

She reached his body and saw the bear trap, the steel jaws digging into the flesh and bone of his front leg. She bent down there was blood everywhere was he dead, she shook this limp body crying out.

"Wake up Daniel it's me Stuti."

The wolf opened its eyes slowly and looked at her, its tongue came out of its mouth and he tried to lick her hand, she moved it closer and felt his dry tongue licking at her hand, tears welled up in her eyes. She put her hands on either side of the steel trap and pulled with all her might but it would not move, she did not have the strength to do it on her own. She saw a shape on his good other front leg and looked closely, she moved the fur with her fingers and saw the tattoo of her name, and it really was Daniel.

The legend had come true once more, she began to sob.

==

She took the wolf's head in her arms and sat down with him and waited, the daylight began to fade and the full moon came into view. The wolf howled she could feel its body getting hot, the heat was intense and she let go of the wolf and went back a few paces on her knees. She saw the fur go back into its body and the arms and back legs straighten out and extend, in the light from the full moon she saw Daniel lying on the grass in the steel trap.

She returned to him and took him in her arms and smiled down at his face, he was so weak and tired. She bent down and kissed him on the lips and said to him.

"I know I'm pregnant Daniel it's like the legend, and I will make sure your son knows all about you."

There was a dry rattle as he managed the words, "Thank you Stuti."

And then, "I love you."

She kissed him again on the lips, and was that a group of men she could hear in the distance growing louder, she wasn't sure.

"I love you, Daniel."

He smiled at her and said, "At least I can die as a man."

And closed his eyes but he was still breathing just, she was sure she could hear men getting closer; she held him close and prayed for a miracle. (2013)

The end

ELEVEN

Leeches

1

The Hudson chemical plant had been it seemed around forever the great funnels lifted into the sky line like huge sentinels reaching up for the clouds. Now as far as anyone knew the company paid for the removal of its waste and this was true to a certain extent, but the removal cost a lot of money and it was cheaper to dump a little amount, an amount no one would notice. That's were Ernie came in he had worked for the company for forty years and now he was retired at sixty-six, but the company paid him to remove the little bit of waste saving them a lot of money.

Ernie knew what he was doing was illegal but the money helped, his pension wasn't a great deal, and it meant he and his wife could go on their annual holidays abroad, this year they had booked up to go to Malaga in Spain. He was a short man and with a bald gleaming head, but he was well liked down the local boozer and that's where he was going in a moment, he drove the van with the six barrels of waste in the back. The barrels were small about double the size of a large paint pot, the company had told him at the start that he was to bury them deep in the woods and he had done this for a few years, but now he was getting old and he found the best place was the sewers.

He stopped the van and climbed out into the chilly night air, it was colder than expected for this time of year in Surrey, March and they were talking about more snow they had enough in January and February. Ernie opened the back door and picked up the first barrel, luckily, they were quiet light. He walked it over to the man hole cover he was parked in a quiet industrial estate at this time of night it was dead perfect for this job.

He got out his pliers and opened the seal round the top, he poured the green goo into the sewer, and he repeated this with all six, and then put the barrels back into the van. Next stop was the local dump it was closed of course, but there was a section of fence that was loose, he slid the wooden fence across and dumped the barrels onto a huge pile of household waste. He got back into the van another week's load gotten rid of, and now it was to the local pub for a few pints of ale, he drove away from the dump and into the night.

==

The man waited in the bushes looking out onto the empty park, he was hiding near the path way and hoped that someone would come along shortly the night was getting colder. This was going to be a monumental night for Ned Getting because on this night he was going to kill his first victim, the first of many that would have the police working overtime, and the whole country in the grip of fear. He was a man of twenty-eight and of medium height at five foot nine inches and he was slim as a rake, he ate like a horse and never put on weight.

He had dark hair cut short and piercing blue eyes that many people had said were cold eyes and they were right. He had been planning to do this for years, and now that his dog of a girlfriend had left him, he could do just that. He dreamed of being a serial killer and one day when this was all over people would write books about him, and he would be in crime monthly the magazine that he collected.

The sound of footsteps ceased his thoughts and he waited in anticipation, he saw the shadow of the woman and waited until she had passed the bushes. She looked like she was drunk she kept nearly walking off the path way onto the grass. He came up behind her and put the cheese wire around her throat and pulled with all his might, the woman gargled and struggled for a second and then went limp, blood poured down her front from the open wound caused by the sharp cheese wire.

He pulled her into the dark side of the park behind the bushes he removed the cheese wire and a spray of blood caught him on the face, he quickly wiped himself with some rag and then the cheese wire.

Now he leaned over the woman and put his mouth to hers, he sucked hard and could feel her soul going into his body; it filled him with wonder and made him strong. He could feel the strength from the woman pass into him, he leaned back and sighed, he had read in a magazine that you could own a person's soul at the time of death, and now he knew it to be true. He took out a small skull and cross bone pin from his pocket this would be his trade mark, he put the pin into the woman's cheek and stood up. He looked down at the dead woman and felt so strong her soul had been a good one, now was his time and the world would one day know his name.

==

Ned walked out of the park all was quiet no one had seen him, he would now become a ghost, a phantom that killed and then disappeared, the police would never find him. He walked down the quiet streets and turned into the trading estate, he looked about no one was about he lifted the man hole cover and climbed down the ladder closing the cover after him. He shone his flash light and walked down the sewer tunnel, he saw lots of green slimly stuff, he paused and looked at it.

"What the fuck is that," he said to himself but shrugged and carried on, just to the left of the tunnel was a steel door built into the tunnel. He got out a key and opened the door and went inside, this was his new home now somewhere no one would find him. He locked the door and turned on the light, it was strange but he had gotten the key off his old man who had worked in the sewer for years.

He was retired now but he had never returned the key and he told Ned what it was for so Ned had stolen it from his draw. It was a place the men used to have a rest or a cup of tea in the old days, but now it was not used and had been largely forgotten. The room had a bed over one side of the wall and a small fridge an over head light and a small cupboard by the bed. He had stocked up the fridge mainly with tins and had put a few of his clothes in the cupboard. Of course, he would go up top and shower every few days, there was a large opening into a stream not to far up so he didn't have to use the man hole cover.

Ned was pleased with his first kill, and couldn't wait to read what the papers had to say about it.

2

The large policeman looked down at the body in the park, Colin Manners was forty-two and drank like a fish, his big beer belly a monument to that. He was going bald on the front and his brown hair would soon disappear altogether. As he looked at the young woman's body, he had a weird feeling the woman looked similar to his ex-wife, but he shook his head why did he have to think about her. She had run off with his best friend three years ago it was lucky they had no kids. Damn he worked to long hours for kid's maybe that's why she had left him, and his drinking of course, she now had a baby from his former best friend that made him feel even shittier.

"What's the verdict," he said to the man working on the body.

"Killed with what looks like cheese wire and then there is this, Colin."

Colin reached down took the plastic bag, he looked inside and saw the skull and cross bone pin.

"Looks like we got ourselves a serial killer."

==

Ned had a restless night in the small sewer room, the soul from the woman had made him excited and sleep was almost impossible, but he had drifted off in the early hours of the morning. Now he needed a shower he would go to his parent's house, they thought he had his own bedsit and said that he could use the shower as he had to share his, and most of the time there was no hot water.

He opened the steel door and stepped into the sewer tunnel, it was always dark down here, he switched on his flash light and moved down the tunnel, God what was that awful smell, and he put his hand to his nose.

The green slim was still there but a lot of it had gone washed away by the water, he moved down the tunnel and shone his light over to another tunnel that branched away to the right. He could have sworn he saw a dark shadow moving away into the tunnel. Damn he was seeing things now, he moved on and stopped, he shone his light down and saw a black long object, puzzled he looked closer and saw the thing rise up and wave in the air, it was a damn leech.

He moved on the leech had spooked him, where they meant to be that long, he thought they were only small, he saw the light of day from the end of the tunnel and sighed with relief. He made his way out and climbed the grassy bank to the top of the road.

==

Alex Roberts moved through the dark sewer, he was thirty-three and a large man at six three with huge shoulders. He liked to work out down the local gym, he hated his job but it paid the rent, and with a wife and two kids to support he couldn't afford to lose it. Damn bloody old timers, there had been two calls this morning complaining about green sludge coming out of peoples drains, now it was his job to look around the sewer in that area and report any sign of green smelly sludge.

He turned into a tunnel and stopped his flash light had caught a large shape in front which quickly disappeared up the tunnel, what the hell was that. Then the smell hit him, he put his hand to his nose, and then brought out his handkerchief, he ran his hand through his thick brown hair and looked straight ahead he couldn't see anything.

He thought about what his wife of five years would be doing now, probably feeding the little ones and then sitting in front of the television drinking tea, alright for some he thought.

He stepped forward's and stopped he had stepped on something; he looked down at his boot, and saw something long and black sticking to it. He pulled the thing off and held it up to the flash light, it was a leech but it was bigger than it should be, he dropped the squashed thing in disgust and walked on.

He stopped on one of the pipes that ran over head he saw another leech; it was waving about in front of him like a cobra snake. He heard a splashing sound in the water and looked down, and the sewer was filled with long black objects. Then the one in front of him on the pipe launched itself at him, he cried out as the thing stuck to his cheek, he gripped the thing and pulled, but it was painful and he stopped the thing was stuck fast.

He felt more leeches crawling up his legs under his trousers and he cried out as the leeches attached themselves to his bare legs. He staggered about putting his hands on the walls to stop himself falling over, but he was feeling weak and the leech on his face had attached its other end to his chin it was feeding from both ends. Alex fell to his knees and then fell face first into the water, more leeches raced through the water to have their fill of him.

3

This was turning into a nightmare, but thankfully Colin had not been required to go down into the sewer, he hated dark confined places. The body of the sewer worker had been found that evening after he failed to turn up, they had gone looking for him and found him down in the tunnels beneath the trading estate. Colin looked at the body before it was loaded into the waiting ambulance, the man was a big man in life he could tell by the size of his shoulders, but his face was all pulled inwards as if he had no blood in his body and there were two Y shaped marks on his cheek and chin. The body was put into the ambulance and the ambulance drove away without using its siren.

He turned to the small man standing close by, he had been called in when the doctor couldn't say what had been the cause of death, and he was something to do with insects or some such crap.

"Looks like we have vampires,' he said to the short man with glass and a bald head, he had a round pleasant face and smiled at Colin.

"Yes, we have and you had better get the garlic flowers out and make sure every carpenter can make wooden stakes it's going to be a busy few days."

Colin looked at the small man, was he serious and then he saw the man brake into a wide grin.

"Sorry for my humor I'm Dan Cherry."

Colin found himself smiling at the little man and took his hand, "Colin I'm in charge of a serial killer case, and just trying to see if this is number two."

"Well, if the first killing was leeches then yes this is number two."

"Leeches did you say leeches."

"Yes, Colin this sewer worker," he looked at his notes and went on, "Alex Roberts was killed by leeches a strain that appear to be bigger than normal but leeches never the less."

"Fucking leeches," was all Colin could say.

"Yes, it's not the first recorded death by leeches, but of course the others happened in the jungles of the world not in a sewer in a city."

"So, what do we do," Colin was stumped this was way out of his league, he was dealing with a serial killer not bloody leeches excuse the pun.

"You look for your serial killer Colin leave this to me and the sewer company."

==

Ned waited this time inside the underground train tunnel, there was a large recess next to him, and if a train came, he would just step into it and wait. There were three people on the platform and it was getting late, he was waiting for one person to be on the platform, and then he would strike for killing number two. It had been a shitty day after his shower his mother had made him breakfast and then his old man had come down.

At first, he was cool, but soon it was what are you doing, I heard you left your job, are you taking drugs why did your girlfriend leave you are you gay, and it went on and on. He finished his breakfast and quickly made his exit with his dad shouting out of the door after him, he wished he could kill his old man but that would be no fun, and he didn't want his dad's soul inside him.

He could still feel the dead woman's soul inside him from the park, it made him feel good and calm, another soul was just what he needed. He stepped back into the recess and waited while another train went by, he waited a few seconds and stepped out and looked at the platform, a single man sat reading a newspaper. Ned walked out of the tunnel and climbed onto the platform the man reading the paper never noticed him; he slowly walked up to the man and coughed.

"Excuse me sir but do you have the time please.'

The man dropped down his paper and looked at him, he wore glasses and had a pointy face he was quite young, and he looked down at his watch. Ned brought out the length of cooper pipe and hit the man hard over the head, the man fell from the seat onto his knees holding his head and moaning, Ned hit him again and again. The man slumped forward onto the platform, Ned quickly turned him over and checked him, there was no pulse he was dead. Ned leaned forward and put his mouth on the dead man's mouth, and sucked hard.

He could feel the man's soul rushing into his body it felt so good and made him feel light as if getting other peoples souls made his own lighter, and all his stress cleared away like dissolving steam. He took out a skull and cross bone pin and put it into the dead man's cheek, number two, and how the papers had loved number one. It seemed that one reporter somehow had got the story about the pin, but had not disclosed details that would just pave the way for copy cats. He was famous and he loved it they were all waiting for number two and he had now given it to them.

==

He walked to the edge of the road all was quiet and then he slipped over the low fence and made his way down the embankment to the sewer entrance by the stream. He couldn't be bothered to walk all the way to the trading estate and use the man hole cover. He waited for a few seconds he remembered the long leech he had seen earlier and shuddered were they meant to be that long. He had asked that question before and moved into the sewer, he turned on his flash light and began to slowly walk it wasn't that far he would be there soon.

He shone his flash light down and saw a long black object it was waving its long body in front of him, he kicked at the thing in disgust. The leech attached itself to his trousers, he reached down and grabbed hold of it, he held it in front of his face and saw the thing twist round and attaches its sucker to his hand, he tried to shake it off but it was stuck fast.

He smashed his hand against the wall and the thing exploded in a splatter of blood, he pulled the dead thing off his hand and cried out, it had ripped a small hole in his hand. He felt something crawling up the inside of his trousers and cried out again as he felt suckers go into his legs, he shone his light down and saw the water filled with leeches.

He ran blindly for his door and quickly inserted the key, he was inside and quickly closing the door, the leeches couldn't get through steel. He quickly took off his trousers and saw two leeches attached to his right leg; he got a pen knife and carefully put it into the sucker and twisted. It was painful, but the thing fell off he did the same to the other one and stamped on the long black bodies on the floor until they were mangled bloody messes. He checked all his clothes and boots no more leeches, he had been lucky, but what the hell were they and why would they attack him. He felt exhausted and his hand throbbed, he lay down on his bed and closed his eyes, killer leeches was his last thought before falling into a deep sleep.

4

Little Timmy screwed up his face and growled at his two friends, they were playing monsters on the embankment.

Little Jilly and Alan shouted and ran off as the monster chased them.

Jilly's blonde hair flew from her face as she ran laughing towards the large sewer opening which ran into the stream.

Timmy tagged Alan who had a crew cut and because his hair was blonde it looked like he was bald, Timmy had a mop of brown hair and he brushed it back from his face as at last someone else was the monster.

"Look at this," Jilly said standing still by the sewer tunnel opening.

"What now Jilly," Timmy said walking over to her.

"Hey it's not fair you two have to run," Alan whined.

Timmy got to where Jilly was and looked down, coming out of the tunnel were long black things, they were like snakes. One of the things rose up and waved in the air as if it were trying to smell them out.

"Snakes," said Timmy.

"No not snakes they have no eyes," Jilly replied.

Alan joined them and looked, "They look like giant leeches, I know because one attached itself to me on holiday once and my dad had to get it off."

They both looked at Alan with this new information.

"Wow giant leeches cool," said Timmy.

As they all watched more and more came out of the sewer tunnel, some went into the stream others made their way onto the grass on the embankment, they were coming towards the three children.

"Let's move away I don't like this," Jilly said taking a step back.

"No way I'm going to catch one," Timmy walked over to the wriggling leeches on the grass. Alan joined him and bent down too.

"So cool but be careful get them with a stick or something," Alan said to Timmy.

But it was too late one of the leeches reared up and attached itself to Timmy's hand. He cried out and looked at the thing on his hand in horror. Jilly screamed and Alan shouted, "Let's get out of here."

Ted was sixty-two and he lived on his own since his dear wife had died ten years ago, but he still missed her to this day, he had no more hair left on his bald head, and had to wear false teeth.

He walked along the road besides the embankment he had just been to the pub and was feeling a wee bit tipsy, he heard the girls scream and then a boy shouting something. Now Ted had never been a hero of any kind, but he was over the small fence that went round the embankment, and he slowly made his way down the grass side. Two kids ran past him and stopped.

"Please mister help our friend," Jilly said pointing over to the sewer tunnel.

'He had been bitten by a leech mister," the boy told him.

Ted made his way to the tunnel with a smile on his face, leeches indeed he thought. But he saw the young boy waving his hand about and saw the long black thing attached to it, then he saw the black forms on the grass they were surrounding the boy. Ted moved over to the boy and picked him up, the leeches rose up and waved at the old man's legs, and one went up his trouser leg. Ted threw the boy over to the side; he landed on the grass and looked back at the old man.

"Run son, run for your life."

The boy needed no second invitation as he saw the leeches crawling up the old man's trousers. The old man felt pain in his legs as the giant leeches attached themselves to him; he tried to reach down but over balanced and fell on his back side. Leeches crawled over his body, he picked up a few and threw them away but there were too many, they attached to his hands and then some reached his face, one attached itself to his nose and with the other sucker attached it to his eye ball, Ted screamed in agony.

==

Colin couldn't believe this crap as he stood in the autopsy room, the body had been brought in just this afternoon. It was another leech case; bloody killer leeches and I got a serial killer who has killed twice the body on the platform had been found yesterday with the same pin stuck in the victim's cheek. The young boy had a leech on his hand, and the Policeman told Colin who arrived late on the scene that it had been removed safely, leeches could be seen on the grass and coming out of the tunnel it had been an awful sight. He had left the scene and driven to the hospital and waited for the autopsy, but he already knew it was leeches poor old bugger. He walked out of the room, sick of the smell of antiseptic in his nostrils.

"Hello Colin."

He looked around and saw the short leech guy what was his name.

"Dan Cherry Colin," he held out his hand Colin took it.

"Another death by leeches what the hell is going on Dan?"

"I had a chance to look at the leech that attached itself to the boy's hand."

"And."

Dan rubbed his chin, "It's a mutation some kind of chemical which enhanced its growth, there was green sludge in its blood."

"Green sludge."

"Yes, whatever this leech digested made it grow and changed its habits it seems."

"Okay."

Dan looked at Colin and said, "Leeches are amazing creatures Colin they have both male and female reproduction organs, they will lay in a long line and one or more leeches will ejaculate sperm over them thus impregnating them all at once. No one knows how long these creatures live, but it's thought around twenty years, but there are different species.

They have three sharp incisors which bury into the skin causing a Y shape mark, if pulled off a leech could cause infection in the wound you have to carefully pry loose with a knife or sharp object."

"Wow that was some lesson thank you doctor."

"Colin, we got to kill these leeches now before anyone else dies."

Colin nodded his head the serial killer could wait these things had to be stopped.

5

Ned lay on his bed and slowly came too, he looked towards the steel door what the hell was that sound, he wearily got to his feet he needed to eat and drink something. He went to the fridge first and took out a can of mixed fruit that would kill two birds with one stone; he opened the can and drank the juice then began to eat the fruit. He looked again at the door way, bits of cement were on the floor, how could that be, he moved closer and got on his knees and looked at the bottom of the door. The cement was being pushed inwards as if something were burrowing into the cement.

Then he saw that the cement was wet from years of water rushing by, the leeches were pushing the wet cement inwards. He got to his feet as he saw the first leech pock its end out of the hole in the cement. He moved back to the bed and sat down putting his legs up, what was he to do now.

==

Colin stood by the sewer tunnel on the embankment, he was with Dan and two other men, the men wore white suits as did he and Dan, the men had flame throwers and held the nozzles out in front of them. Colin moved to the entrance of the sewer; leeches were still pouring out of the sewer tunnel how many were there for Christ's sake. As he watched the two men began to torch the long black things, they sizzled as the flames covered their bodies, black smoke went up into the air, Colin was glad he was wearing a Hemet with an air filter.

"There are so many Dan how do we kill them all, and a lot of them are going into the stream.'

There was a radio inside the helmet and it was set to talk to all three men, each could hear what the others were saying.

"I don't know yet Colin I will think of something for the stream."

"Seems to have stopped sir," said one of the flame throwers soldiers.

Colin saw what he meant the burning leeches in the tunnel were the only things there no more seemed to be coming out.

"Looks like we stopped them Dan."

Dan shook his head in the helmet, "No Colin they will find some other way out now we need to go in and blast them."

The four men in white suits entered the sewer tunnel with Dan leading the way; each man had a flash light built into the top of his helmet.

==

Dan stepped slowly over the dead burning leeches and moved into the darkness of the tunnel, he could see up ahead a line of leeches moving away from them, no doubt looking for another way out.

He stopped.

"Right one of you guys goes in front as soon as you see leeches burn them on sight.'

One of the soldiers took the lead the other took the rear.

"Okay sir.'

They walked on and passed a steel door, Dan stopped even through the helmet he could hear screams coming from inside the door, and it must be some kind of room.

"Colin come here I can hear screaming."

Colin came to the door and leaned against it, "Your right Dan, I can hear them to."

"Right, you in front carry on and torch the fuckers you at the rear come with me and Colin," Dan was good at giving the orders thought Colin to himself.

"Kick the door in soldier," Dan told him the door was locked from the inside.

==

Ned screamed as the leeches came into the room, they slithered across the floor towards the bed, as if they knew where he was straight away. A line of leeches stopped by the bed and rose up and waved in front of the bed as if trying to work out how to get the man on top of it. Ned screamed again as the leeches began to climb up the bed legs, one reached the blanket by him, he quickly brought down his fist on the thing, black and green slime erupted out of the black body. He looked at his hand in discussed and vomited all over the floor, some of the fruit cocktail covered the leeches, but they just moved onwards to the bed, there were hundreds of the things.

==

The door was old and the heavy-set soldier stepped back, they could now see the leeches going under the doorway. The soldier kicked the door and it came away from the hinges the door crashed to the cement floor. They entered the room stepping on the steel door and crushing loads of the leeches on the bed was a man screaming and crying. Leeches were all over the bed legs and moving up towards him. Dan motioned for the man to jump on the steel door.

The man understood and got into a kneeling position and jumped, Colin caught him and they both fell onto the steel door, Colin quickly regained his feet even for a big man he moved fast in danger. The four men stood on the steel door and the soldier let the leeches on the bed have it, a long line of flames shot out and covered the bed.

They watched the sizzling leeches then Colin happened to look at the side board, he moved closer and grabbed the wooden cabinet and pulled it away from the flames. There in a plastic cup were pins with skull and cross bones on them, Colin looked at the man and couldn't believe his luck. Ned saw the large man holding up the plastic cup of pins the game was up. It was all over he just wanted to be away from this hell hole.

"It's me I am the killer please just get me out of here please," the man sobbed at Colin.

6

Later that day another team of soldiers with flame throwers were sent into the tunnels after two hours they came out. They had killed thousands, but no one was sure if that was all of them, there had just been too many. As for the stream it was closed off to the public, a metal fence surrounded the stream until they decided what to do about the leeches in it. Dan went back to his work in Leeds taking a few live leeches with him; he was going to find out the best way to kill the remaining leeches in the water.

==

Colin looked at the piece of shit sitting across from him his arms resting on the wooden table; he leaned back in his chair.

"So, you hide in the sewer and come up and kill your victims."

The man Ned drank his strong black coffee he was still shaking from the encounter with the leeches.

"Yes, I told you everything; do with me as you please."

'It was lucky for us that these leeches decided to kill don't you think so Ned.'

The man laughed at that, "Yes it was you would never have found me in the sewers if it wasn't for them damned leeches."

"Very true you would have killed a lot more people you sick fuck."

He paused and looked Ned in the eyes, "I should have fed you to those leeches you sick motherfucker."

The man started to laugh again.

"What the fuck are you laughing at?"

Now Colin could feel the rage rise in his body, and he clenched his fists.

"I'm sorry officer but it's not just leeches you have to worry about.'

"What do you mean by that?"

The man was silent for a moment pondering whether to tell or not and then he said, "I have seen giant shadows in them tunnels I kid you not."

"Shadows like what."

"Giant rats."

Now it was Colin's turn to laugh.

==

The soldier was bored he had been walking around in the sewer tunnels for hours, this was the last sweep he had been told. Jerry wanted out now he was sick of the dark tunnels, and he hadn't seen a single leech in two hours, he held the nozzle out in front of him and walked on. When he got back to base it was his night off and he would go into town and get drunk, and pull some old slapper and fuck the brains out of her, yes that seemed like a good plan to him. He was a soldier for fuck's sake and couldn't remain faithful, and besides Kerry would never find out.

He loved her and he knew that she was waiting for him to finish his remaining two years, and then set up home. He did want that but while he could he would enjoy, he stopped as he saw the water up ahead move was that a leech. He walked over and tilted his head so the light fell on the water's surface; it was a leech alright the first one he had seen for ages, he straightened up and pointed the nozzle down at the leech.

Something big came out of the shadows, he screamed and dropped the nozzle as he felt sharp teeth bite into his sides, and blood gushed out of his moth, and covered the helmet screen inside. The powerful jaws locked down on his body, and carried it away into the sewer tunnels. (2013)

The end

TWELVE

Who is the wolf?

Prologue

The white man wiped sweat from his brow and looked across the mountains to the valleys below, they had been trekking up the mountains for days now, and the Hindi crush was a vast mountain range. The man kicked at a loose rock and it went flying down the steep incline in front of him, one of his Indian helpers stopped by his side.

"We go on boss."

The white man nodded his head and looked down at the small Indian guide, he wasn't racist, but they all looked the same to him, they had thick black hair and dark eyes, all four helpers must be brothers or related in some way.

"Yes, let's move on before night fall."

There was a rumor that a small boy lived in the caves of the Hindi crush and that the boy was more animal than human, the white man was searching for him, but he was beginning to wonder if this was all a waste of time. He liked an adventure but now he was getting bored.

==

They made camp close to set of caves, they would search the caves in the morning, the white man lay on the top of his sleeping bag, it was far too hot to climb inside a lantern hung from the hook in the metal pole of the tent. He would search the caves and then call a halt to the adventure, and get back to the village to finish off his time in India. He closed his eyes and heard a sound outside of his tent, he pulled his head up and looked, but he couldn't see through the canvas tent. He moved to the opening and drew up the zipper, all was dark outside

He saw the remains of the fire from earlier where one of the guide's had cooked a meal for them all, he could make out three shapes sleeping on the hard ground, the fourth he could not see. The shape came out of the darkness with a roar, he was frozen in fear, next he felt a sharp pain on his cheek and felt his blood running down his face, the thing had clawed him.

Then a shot rang out in the darkness, the fourth helper fired at the dark shadow and the shadow disappeared, the white man held his cheek. The helper walked over to him rifle in his hand.

"We go back tomorrow morning boss not safe here."

The white man nodded at him in the dark.

Indian moon

The full moon was high in the night sky as the young Indian man smoked a cigarette outside his tin hut, he had built the hut himself from sheets of tin, and he could hear the television inside as his wife watched her Indian soap operas. He lived in a small village just on the out skirts of a town, the rest of the homes were made up of tin sheets like his own, and some were made of mud and bricks.

He heard a noise off to his left and looked over at the sound and relaxed it was only a small boar sniffing through some waste on the ground, the village was full of boars.

They probably outnumbered the humans and they were part of the village, and the two seemed to get along fine mainly staying out of each other's way. The boar moved into the bush, he threw his cigarette onto the ground and was just turning to go inside his hut when he heard a sound coming from the bushes. The boar squealed and then went silent he moved closer to the bush and then hell erupted into his face.

He didn't have time to scream as the furry face was pushed into his own, he felt a terrible pain in his abdomen and looked down, his intestines were falling out of his stomach he tried to push them back in with his hands. He fell to his knees moaning and the beast took an almighty swing at his head, the clawed hand severed the head from the shoulders. The head flew into the tin hut the body fell on its front blood pumping out of the stump of the neck.

The woman looked up from the television screen and looked to her right something had rolled into the hut. There was only one room in the hut and that's where they did everything, the floor was covered in blankets to hide the dirt underneath. At first, she thought the object was a football, some of the teenagers in the village played football, then she saw her husband looking at her, the torn flesh of his severed neck still shiny with his blood. His mouth hung open and he stared straight ahead, terror in his eyes, the woman screamed, and then the huge shape leapt into the side of the hut.

The tin sheet was no match for the force of the beast and it collapsed inwards falling on top of the woman. She was under the tin sheet and could fell the weight of the animal as it stepped on her, then the weigh was gone and the sheet was thrown to one side. She screamed again as she looked into the dark green eyes of the beast.

==

The second night of the full moon and the disco sounds boomed out from the night club, the bouncer moved into the darkness of the alley way, the place would not let any more people into night so it was time for a smoke. He had made one earlier from the weed he had at home, and now lit the joint and took a deep inhale and closed his eyes, bliss. Having a night club in town really helped, the Indian youngsters came from miles around to dance and drink at the club.

The bouncer sighed as he took another drag, he wasn't a big man in fact he didn't look hard at all, but he had been an amateur boxer for many years, and knew how to handle himself. He heard a deep breathing coming from somewhere in the alley way. He moved farther into the dark alley.

"Hey who is there?"

The shadow came out of the dark and hit him head on, he fell backwards with the force and hit his head on the concrete. He saw white spots before his eyes, but his vision cleared and he got up on his elbow and rubbed the back of his head.

"Fuck what was that.'

Then from behind jaws clamped around the back of his neck, jaws like steel traps and crushed his neck until the head rolled across the ground, blood sprayed over the walls of the night club's side. The beast began to feed on the bouncer's carcass.

English moon

Barry kissed his girlfriend on the mouth and slipped his tongue into hers, she pulled away from him.

"Why do we have to do it here Barry?"

They were in the local cemetery and laying on top of a marble grave the marble cross at the end throwing shadows on them.

"I like it its cool."

"Making out on a grave in a cemetery is cool."

She sat up and adjusted her top, he looked longing at her huge breasts, and he was getting so hard now. He had seen her breasts the week before after the movie, she had showed him and they were lovely he had been wanking over the thought of them all week, and now she was going to go.

"Don't go Mindy please," he whined at her.

"I have to get back home," she said in a voice that had no room for argument. The shape came out of nowhere, one minute she was tiding herself up and the next she was gone. He looked at the empty space and couldn't work out what the hell had happened something had grabbed her that was obvious. He stood up and dumbly walked round the graves looking for her.

"Mindy, Mindy where are you."

He heard a noise over to his right and looked, there was a wooden fence that separated the cemetery from the orchard on the other side, and he walked over and climbed the wooden fence. He could smell the apples on the trees as he walked between them, he stopped and looked at the shape on the ground, and it was Mindy or what was left of her. Her clothes had been torn off and one of her breasts was missing, blood pumped up from the blood wound, her throat had been torn out and one of her feet was missing. He looked at the brown triangle between her legs in the light from the moon, so that's what she looked like naked, he laughed as he heard a sound from behind, but he didn't care anymore.

==

"Wait a second,' the big boy said to his two companions.

They were hiding behind some bricks in the dump; they had been waiting for hours and so far, no sign of the wankers. The gang was called the 'Howlers' and the big guy was the leader, Ricky loved being in charge it made he feel like a big man, he looked at his two gang members and smiled at them.

"I think they are chicken shit guys."

They were meant to be meeting for a fight at the dump with the 'terrors' a rival gang. Normally there were five members in the 'howlers' but two had not been able to make it, but Ricky didn't care three would be enough to beat the 'terrors.'

All three lads had their hair shaved bald and wore black leather coats with the words the 'howlers' on the back and a picture of a snarling wolf.

"Fuck it Rick lets go."

"Yeah man they aint going to show now," his two friends moaned at him.

"Just a little bit longer guys okay trust me they will show."

Then they all heard the noise coming from the left of the dump, it was the noise of a steel sheet being lifted and something moving inside, they gang had come at last. Ricky reached into his pocket and took out a knuckle duster, he put it on his hand and his two friends took out metal bars and held them ready.

"Okay when I gave the order, we rush them okay lads.'

The two other boys said together, "Yes."

Ricky tensed himself he saw a shape move through some bushes this was going to be so fucking good he thought, he clenched his fist tight. The shadow came into the moon light and Ricky gasped, the huge animal stopped and looked Ricky right in the eye.

Ricky soiled his pants and ran, he left his two mates behind, he ran blindly and ran right slam bang into a tree. Knocking himself out cold and he lay on the ground a slight wound on the top of his forehead, blood ran down in a tiny trickle. The beast jumped on the two lads, knocking one over to the right on the hard ground, the other boy it took in its jaws, it clamped its jaws round the kids' leg, the boy cried out in pain.

The beast flicked its head roughly and the left leg tore away from the boy's body, he screamed and fell to the floor holding his stump, blood rushing through his fingers. The beast turned and clawed the other boy across the face, tearing half his face off, the boy moaned and was about to scream, but it was cut off as the beast took out his throat with another swing of its clawed hand.

Ricky opened his eyes, what the hell had happened then it all came back to him, he got up on his elbows and looked around in the dark, he couldn't hear anything. Maybe the thing had gone; he could feel the wetness in his under pants, but was too scared to feel ashamed. Then he got up into a sitting position and looked straight in front of him, the beast was an inch away from his face, the fowl breath hitting him. He screamed as the beast took his face in its jaws and twisted, his neck snapped like a twig.

Later the gang the 'terrors' turned up at the dump, there were four of them and they were armed with baseball bats, it wasn't long before they found the chewed up remains of the 'howlers' and the then main sound in the dump was puking and screaming.

The suspects

The office was a mess but Ray didn't care that's the way he liked it, the spate of killings over the last two nights had his superiors worried it looked like some sort of serial killer. A manic for sure, how could a man rip bodies apart like that, he had to be crazy and strong as hell. Ray was thirty-two and single, and had been so since his girlfriend had left him because he was never home, which was true he was married to the police force, and he loved it.

He was a thin tall man with ginger hair cut short; he didn't need to shave because no hair ever grew on his chin or upper lip which saved him money. He had been to the arsenal football match yesterday evening, and had missed the gang killings until this morning; three kids ripped apart found by a rival gang, they were probably going to rumble. The 'terrors' had been allowed to go home there was no way on this planet that those four kids could have done this, and besides that they were clean not a drop of blood on them. His door opened and he smiled as his boss walked in.

"Hello Ray how are you good to be back."

He smiled again he had just got back from holiday a few days ago.

"Yes, boss it's good to be back."

The fat man smiled in front of him and said, "So when are you going climbing in India again."

"Hope to go again soon boss."

==

The class was almost over and Ernie was glad, he was feeling extra tired today, and wanted to go home and rest. One of the young girls in the front row winked at him and smiled at him, damn she was good looking, and young Jennifer had always had a crush on him. She was thirteen as were all the kids in this class, she always brought him apples and oranges, and sometimes even chocolate. She brushed her long blonde hair away from her eyes and smiled at him once more. He was a history teacher and enjoyed his job even with teenage crushes. The bell went and not a moment too soon for him.

"Okay no homework for today, but I will give you extra next week so be warned."

The kids poured out of his class room and young Jennifer put an apple on his desk and said sexily to him, "Bye sir have a good weekend," and then she was gone shaking her little as butt as she went.

Ernie was a single man he had been married once, but it was a mistake they were at each other's throats from day one and it had lasted a year. But he liked being on his own and sometimes going to the local pub at the weekends, and talking to his mates about football mainly he was a huge arsenal fan. He had sandy hair tied back in a pony tail and he wore glasses, but he had a rugged face and woman found him attractive. He looked up as the door opened and the school principal walked in.

"Great job as always Ernie."

"Sorry sir what."

"The pictures you took of India great job everyone loves them."

He had put a load of his pictures from his trip to India recently on the bulletin board for everyone to see.

"I'm so glad people liked them sir."

==

Matthew held his girlfriend's hand as they walked down the high street, the night was a warm one for a change they had so much rain lately. He was a rugby player and played for his local team he was hoping to make it into the professional ranks one day soon, and make a living out of that which he loved so much. He was a tall young man at nineteen, but he looked a lot older than his years, people often mistook him for mid twenties.

He had black hair which was brushed back Robert DeNiro style and had a day's growth of beard it made him look rugged his girlfriend would often say which he liked.

"Movie should be good tonight," he said as they walked past the pizza hut restraint.

"I don't know it's a horror you know I get scared Matt."

He squeezed her hand and smiled in the darkness, "Don't worry love you can hide behind me when it gets too scary," he laughed.

She stopped and he stopped with her, he looked at her and she smiled.

"Please take me with you next time Matt."

"Take you where."

"You know where you scum bag," she joked with him.

"I want to go with you to India next time you go please say yes."

He had been to India recently and she had not been able to go because of her studies, "Okay Linda I promise."

==

The shop had been quiet today so Justin had let his assistant Lucy go home early he would close up the shop. Lucy was a good girl she had looked after the shop while he had been away and done a sterling job, he had paid her extra, and she was happy with that. She was a good-looking girl and he knew all the young boys were after her some of them came into the shop just to talk with her.

Justin had owned the shop nearly all his life, when his parents had died, he had invested the money in this paper come sweet shop, and for the past fifteen years it had been doing well. He was forty-three and as bald as a coot, he wore steel rimmed glasses and looked more like a professor than a store owner. The door opened and in came Miss Gold; she was a regular and a chatter box.

'Hello Justin so good to see you again how was India this time."

He smiled at her and replied, "India was good as always."

More killings and a hideaway

His shift was finished and Ray was glad to get away from the office, night time would fall soon and he was looking forward to just chilling out and watching the television. He had bought himself a nice steak for dinner tonight and with door step chips he was going to enjoy he liked his steaks rare. He smiled at a kid pushing himself along on his scooter his mother close behind and looking hassled.

Matt dropped Linda off at her home she still lived with her parents, but they were looking to settle down once their studies were over. He kissed her on the lips.

"Bye honey see you tomorrow."

"What are you going to do this evening?"

He smiled at her and winked, "I'm going for a long bike ride."

He pushed off and rode the bike down the street. Linda looking until he disappeared around a bend.

Ernie unlocked his front door and walked into his small living room, it was almost night time and he could see the full moon coming up from his window. He moved inside and took off his shoes he was dead beat after walking around town, he was going for a pint but in the end he didn't bother. He sat on the settee and closed his eyes.

He smiled at Lucy as he made his way out of the shop.

"See you tomorrow, Lucy."

"Bye Justin have a nice evening."

Oh, I will he smiled and thought to himself, he was having an early day tonight. Lucy didn't mind closing up for him. He could see that it was getting darker the full moon would be up soon.

==

The man walked quickly down the street, looking into every shadow he was sure that he was being followed, he had the feeling two streets ago. He had just been taking his merry time and out of the corner of his eye he saw a shadow in the darkness, always keeping hidden in the dark alleys, but it was there and he knew it.

Keith Mann was a shameless soul, he enjoyed making people squirm and as he was manager of a large chain of fast-food restaurants, he had loads of opportunities to do it. He had lots of kids just working for the summer holidays before college the little bastards he made them work for their damn money, and then there was the blacks and the Indians. He couldn't stand them and made no bones about that he didn't like them. Put them all on a boat and send them back to where they came from that's what he would do if he was in the government.

He saw the shape again this time way down in an alley way, he saw it move the shape was big no doubt about that. He walked on he would have to go through the park soon, it was the only quick way to get home, and home for Keith was a studio flat. He was an ugly man with loads of spots on his face and as white as a sheet he had heard the nick names at work the ghost man, and potato head he didn't think his head was shaped like a potato, but bloody kids.

He was twenty-nine and had never had a girlfriend; he stayed away from the opposite sex and found that he was clumsy and accident prone in front of them. He stopped by the entrance to the park, he took a deep breath, and moved into the dark park there was no way he was going to take the long route damn that would add another twenty minutes to his journey. The Park was silent and he walked quickly he heard a breathing sound from behind him; he stopped and looked into the trees.

"Hello is any one there."

Then he heard the sound from behind him the thing had back tracked him, he turned quickly.

"Look dick head this is not funny."

Then the shape came out of the darkness like a blur, it hit him in the chest and pain erupted through his body, he felt his chest and felt where the clothes had been torn, and he could feel the wetness of his own blood. The thing stood over him and he screamed as it drew back its clawed hand and swiped at him.

==

Scott hid in the bushes he was a little fat man with a bald head which was covered with a wooly hat, he was waiting for some girl or woman to walk past. All he wore was a thick grey over coat and some boots on his feet he was a flasher, and got such a kick out of doing it. He was already hard now just thinking about his next victim.

At fifty-five and having a loving wife who was at home and three grown up kids he often wondered why this turned him on so much, if he got caught his wife would be devastated. Then he heard the scream in the park, he looked round it had come from over by where the path bend round a corner, there were a lot of trees over there. He moved out of the bushes now his penis had gone limp, he walked slowly over to where the trees were, and he couldn't see much in the darkness he had left his glasses at home.

The trees were thick and he pushed through them he stepped on something wet and slimly he had almost lost his footing and slipped. He looked down and from the light of the moon saw a man's torso and it had been ripped apart. He said a "Fuck," and then the shape came out of the trees, it hit him hard across the face and he went flying back and smacked into a tree trunk, he slid down and sat watching as the thing approached him.

==

Ray looked at the papers the next day on the front page the police were asking all citizens of the town who had been to India to come forward, it was just an inquiry. He walked into the office and was immediately grabbed by his boss.

"Two more fucking killing last night in Hayden Park."

"Shit man and I missed them again."

"I want you to get over to the park now and just scan the bloody area."

He was going to walk away, but stopped and turned to his fat boss and said, "What about this India thing I've just come back from there."

"Don't worry it's just a hunch seems there were similar killings in India recently, and now they have stopped just wanted to talk to anyone who has been, you never know we might find this loony."

Justin sat down in front of his computer, he had read the paper his morning and had told Lucy to look after things for half hour, he turned on the lap top and went straight into face book. He put a post on his wall asking anyone who had been to India recently to meet him at the railway station this afternoon to discuss what to do about the police harassment. He smiled as he looked at the post, good that should get a few people interested, he would take them to his cabin in the woods just outside town.

He waited at the train station and looked at his watch it was twelve noon dead; he had told face book he would be wearing a red sweater, but of course most people knew him anyway. He saw young Matt and smiled he knew the boy well from his shop in fact he knew everyone, Matt walked over to him.

"I saw your post on face book."

"Good boy I didn't know you had been to India."

"Yes, just got back in fact.'

Then he saw the policeman Ray, he knew him a little and then the teacher Ernie, both walked up to him.

"So, what is all this about," Ray said looking at the shop keeper.

"Just a meeting to see what action we can take this thing with the police is well out of order."

Ray nodded it did seem a bit silly to him.

Ray had decided to go when he saw the post on face book because one it might lead to some clues about the killings it was too good an opportunity miss.

"Okay guys now we go to my cabin to talk this thing out."

"Your cabin," Ernie said.

"Yes, it's the best place quiet and just out of town."

They all followed Justin to his car.

==

The cabin was small but cozy as you walked in you saw the tiny kitchen straight ahead the living room was as you walked in there was a settee and a chair, and an open fire place, two doors were over on the far wall, the two bedrooms.

"Very nice Justin not bad at all mate," said Ernie looking around he sat on the chair.

Ray and Matt sat on the settee and Justin pulled over a wooden chair from the kitchen.

"Yes, nice place," Ray added.

"Thank you it's my little escape at weekends."

"So, what are we going to do about the police hassling us," Matt said staring the conversation. Justin made coffee and sandwiches and they soon got lost in the conversation it switched to different things and then came back on track again, time past and soon the day was turning into night the full moon would be up soon.

The wolf revealed

Night fell quickly outside of the cabin, the men inside where silent now; the full moon started its rise to the top of the night skies. Ernie was nervous as he saw the full moon; he began to sweat and wished that he was at home with a nice cold glass of beer in his hand, and watching television with his feet up.

Matthew wished he was with his girlfriend just going to the cinema or hanging out helping each other with their studies; he missed her and longed for her now. He watched the full moon outside of the cabin through the small glass window.

Justin was dripping in sweat as he watched the full moon outside; he had a bad feeling about this night. He looked at the others the calmest of them all seemed to be the policeman Ray he sat reading the paper and seemed as cool as a cucumber.

Ray looked up from the paper and saw Justin watching him, he smiled at the shop keeper, he needed to pee badly, and the toilet was outside to the right of the cabin.

"Got to pee gentlemen be back in a minute."

"You know how to find it Ray," Justin asked him.

He nodded he had already been once before, "Yes no problem, mate."

He opened the cabin door and stepped out into the night air looking up at the full moon as he closed the door behind him and made his way to the outside toilet.

==

Ray closed the toilet door it was a small wooden shack just big enough for one man to go inside, and the toilet had a tank underneath with liquid that dissolved people's waste. Justin had told them this earlier then every few months he changed it. Ray peed and felt so much better the reason he was so cool was that he was just watching the others for any sign of a disturbed mind; maybe he was sitting with the deranged killer. But the three men had acted and sounded normal, he was barking up the wrong tree.

He zipped himself up and paused for a moment had he heard a noise coming from the cabin, something being knocked over, he cocked his head to one side and listened. He opened the wooden door and stepped out of the toilet he looked up again at the full moon and marveled at its beauty.

He walked round the side of the cabin and stopped the front door was open, he was sure he had closed it when he left. He moved slowly to the door way and looked inside. He choked back his vomit and turned away trying to get his breath back, he took large lung full's of air, he began to sweat.

As he had looked into the cabin, he had seen two mangled bodies they were covered in blood and gore, and it was impossible to see who they were. If he went inside and had a proper look then he could make out who they were. He heard a sound in front of him; he tried to look into the darkness.

The shape came out from nowhere and slashed him across the face, he cried out in pain as he felt his cheek being ripped apart, and then the beast slashed him across the belly, and then the throat. It was blindingly quick and Ray had no time to defend himself, he sank to his knees his intestines falling in steamy piles onto the ground, and blood pumping out of his throat wound. The beast waited until the man had died and then started to feed on his dead body, the beast then went into the cabin and knocked over an oil lamp. The beast sat a distance away and watched the fire for a while, then it looked up at the full moon and howled.

==

The shop door opened and two men walked into the shop, Justin looked up from his paper and smiled at them. The larger of the two showed the shop keeper his badge.

"Just following up on your statement a few days ago sir."

The man looked at his notes.

"You stated that you and three men were having a drink at your cabin when officer Ray Burrows went crazy and killed two of your friends before you knocked him out and accidently set the cabin on fire is that correct sir."

Justin put on a sad looking face, "He was such a good man but to see the way he ripped my friends apart he had abnormal strength yes."

"How did you say you knocked him out," the policeman looked puzzled Ray was twice the size of this guy.

"I got lucky he slipped and fell hitting his head, all I had to do was hit him again to make sure, then I knocked the lamp over."

The policeman nodded the case was closed the bodies had all been identified. Ray was the killer it was hard to believe but all evidence pointed that way now.

"You won't be needing me again officers I take it."

The big policeman shook his head, "No sir this case is closed."

"Good because I'm thinking of taking a holiday to Spain shortly."

He grinned at the men; he could do with getting away for a bit. (2013)

The end

THIRTEEN

The soul collector

The little village in the surrey countryside was expecting snow and people pulled their coats up tight around their throats, it was bitterly cold. The wise old man sat by the duck pond on a wooden bench, the duck pond was in a small square of grass with the parish church almost right next to it. They called Pugh the old wise man instead of a tramp because he would often say wise words to the kids and even the parents, and people listened to him. He had tatty old clothes and hadn't had a bath for a long time, his unkempt white hair and beard would soon blend in with the snow that was on the way. He looked at the ducks in the water and said to himself.

"Something evil is on the way."

==

The shop had been closed down for a good few months and it seemed like no one was ever going to reopen it. The shop had been a green grocer for many years until the man and his wife had sold up and moved to America to be with their grown-up kids. The person who they sold to died in a car accident, and so far, no one in the village knew what was going to happen to the place. The shop stayed boarded up and neglected. A dark shadow fell across the shop window, the sound of nails coming out of wood, and the sound of a door opening and closing, the dark shadow hid everything not that there was anyone about at this late hour. The dark shadow stayed for an hour and then slowly disappeared.

The next day people stopped and starred at the shop, the new looking glass window and the sign above the shop read collector of rare objects. People began to talk it was a small village and soon the whole place was wondering what and who owned the new shop, and how had he got things up and running so quickly.

Robert Elliott was the first person to enter the new shop and that had been luck he had been walking past thinking of who he could whack next when the door opened, and the little bell sounded on top. Robert was eleven years old and was the toughest kid in the school no one messed with him, and he beat up on a kid daily.

He was in truth a spoilt brat and his parents got him whatever he wanted, he always had the latest gadgets and games consoles. He had a crew cut and he was chubby and had a round face and a pug nose, he looked at the open door and walked into the shop.

"Hello master Elliott."

The man behind the counter wore a dark suit and his face was as white as a ghost, he had dark hair swept back on his head and a small neatly trimmed goatee beard, he looked like a predator going after its prey, the little boy shuddered in his presence.

"Lucky your name isn't Bates," and the man laughed.

The boy laughed with him, but he didn't understand the joke at all.

"Look around my boy and see if there is anything you like."

The boy looked at the objects without much interest then his eyes fell on the baseball bat, he loved to watch baseball on cable television. He picked up the bat it was signed by Babe Ruth one of the most famous players in history, little Robert knew all about the baseball history.

"Wow look at this bat."

"It can be yours Robert."

The young boy realized he hadn't told the man his name, but he knew this entire name but that was soon forgotten as he held the bat in his hands looking down at it.

"How much sir."

"For you my little friend your soul."

"My soul sir."

The man grinned at him and said, "Think of all the people you can make jealous at school."

"Yes, that would be so cool."

"Sign here my little friend."

Robert walked over to the counter and signed his name on a sheet of paper inside a large black book.

"There it's yours for three days enjoy."

The man gave Robert a card, the boy put it in his pocket.

==

After three days of showing off with the bat little Robert withdrew the card from his jacket pocket, he had forgotten about it till now. His dad was suspicious of the shop who would loan a bat like that to a kid, but he kept it to himself. He looked down at the card it read the soul collector and the address was the woods stand in front of the line of trees and you will see.

Little Robert went into the woods that evening he found the line of trees and stood there looking as his eyes grew more adjusted, he saw the red curtains between the trees. He walked over and pushed one of the curtains aside and stepped into the void beyond.

He was in a sandy area and he could see sand for miles he looked behind him and only saw sand where was he. Then he saw a shape moving under the sand, it was coming to get him, he knew that it was a monster just like in that movie about giant worms, and then he saw the rocks he raced over to them. He sat panting on the highest rock and a voice behind him said.

"Welcome Robert."

He turned and saw a skinny man sitting a few feet away, he looked like the man in the shop, but older he had grey hair and no goatee beard.

"You have met my brother now you meet me, and I'm a different creature altogether."

"Who are you sir."

The figure laughed and its face changed now it had horns coming out of its head and its chin was long and pointy, its feet were replaced by hoofs.

"I am the soul collector."

Little Robert walked back home but he wasn't the same he walked blindly ahead like a zombie; his little body was now just an empty shell. As he came into the village he waited on the side of the road, then a car came speeding down he stepped off the pavement and into the path of the car.

==

Angie Robinson looked at the vase in wonder, it was so beautiful she had never seen a vase like it before, it had a sort of blue and green haze, and the design had women and men entwined with each other it was a magnificent vase. She smiled and looked at the man behind the counter, he was as white as a sheet, but he was quite handsome with his pointy face and goatee beard.

"How much for the vase sir.'

He smiled at her, "What prices can you put on beauty my dear."

She looked in her hand bag she had about a hundred pounds, she had to have that vase, she would show it off to Linda her neighbor who was always showing off with better things than she. Now it was Angie turn to put this right up her stuck-up nose.

"I have a hundred pounds sir I know it's not much."

The man waved her over to the counter, she stepped up to him and he smiled at her.

"I will loan you the vase for three days if you give me your soul."

She giggled at him, that was just plain silly, but she needed to have that vase.

"Sign here my dear," he held out an old book and she signed her name.

He handed her a card, she looked down read. The soul collector and the address the woods, stand in front of the line of trees and you will see.

Her neighbor drank the tea from the China cup, and looked at the vase for the hundredth time. Angie felt as proud as punch as she saw the jealousy in Linda's eyes. She was loving this moment Linda had made her jealous so many times, and this was to be her sweet revenge.

"It's just so amazing Angie where did you get it."

"Let's just say I picked it up in a store out of town."

There was no way that she was going to tell Linda where she bought the vase.

Linda sat there with her blonde hair all done up nice and she wore far too much make up she would need a trowel to remove all that shit. Angie smiled to herself.

But three days later Angie found herself walking in the woods it was late and she used a flash light to find her way to the line of trees. She stood there, and then she saw the green curtains, waving in the slight breeze between the lines of trees.

She walked over to the curtains and stepped inside. She was in a long white corridor; she looked behind her and saw another long corridor stretching off into the distance. She walked down the corridor and she walked and walked turning corners as she went, this was never ending, then she saw a door painted green her favorite color. She opened the door and stepped inside, a man sat on top of a table, the table was the only furniture in the white washed room. He smiled at her he looked like the man from the shop, but he didn't have a goatee beard.

"Hello my dear," he smiled a wide smile his eyes were the brightest green she had ever seen.

"Hello do I know you sir."

"You meet my brother but I am a totally different creature my dear."

His face changed and his chin became long, his legs rippled and ripped through his trouser he had the legs of a lion, his ribs came out of his chest like sharp spears. She cried out and turned to the door, but there was no door.

Then from behind her came the voice.

"I am the soul collector my dear."

Now just outside of the town there is a big group of hills often used by hikers and campers in the summer time, one of these hills ended in a sear drop. Angie walked to this sear drop like a mindless zombie; her body was but a shell. She stood on the edge of the cliff for a moment, then calmly walked off the edge.

==

Peter Elliot tried to think of what his son had told him before he died something about getting the bat from a shop, the new shop but he had been vague. He was a stocky man and had been an amateur boxer for six years in his youth, he was going to send his son to a boxing gym, but now that was all over.

He was at the new shop he stopped and looked through the window. He could see objects that looked expensive and a dark man standing behind the counter, he entered the shop.

"Please sir look around," the man said waving his hand about, he had a goatee beard and was so white.

Peter wasn't really interested in buying anything; he wanted to know if his son had been in the shop.

"I don't want anything sir."

The man frowned at him, "We can't please everyone."

"My son Robert died last week I want to know if he got a bat from here."

The man rubbed his chin and looked around the shop thinking.

"No sir what could a boy possible afford in my shop."

Then Peter saw the bat, it looked like the one Robert had been showing off to everyone. The man behind the counter saw this.

"I am going to the police."

"Of course, sir you do that I have nothing to hide."

==

Willy went into the shop he had a lot on his mind, his wife of twenty years was having an affair with his best mate, and he had seen them together last week, and was now trying to think what action to take. He loved his wife and didn't want her to leave him, but he had to make his best mate pay some way or the other.

"Please sir look around we are having a closing sale today."

Willy looked at the man behind the counter he was so white he looked like a damn ghost. Willy shifted his feet he was a large man with a wave of curly brown hair, and a huge beer belly. Willy nodded at the man and went round the small shop he stopped and saw the hunting rifle, it had an ivory handle, and there were carved pictures of wolfs on the barrel.

"Wow that is magnificent."

"Yes, sir a very rare hunting rifle indeed."

"How much," Willy spoke sharply he didn't like wasting time.

"For you sir your soul."

He looked at the man in the black suit and laughed, "My soul."

"Yes, sir just sign here."

The man held out an old book.

It had been a great idea, Willy had shown his best mate Larry the rifle and said they should go rabbit shooting, and Larry had agreed, and now they both stood in the woods Larry with his old air rifle. Willy had a real gun and he shifted its weight in his hands, his big beer belly was used as a rest for the gun.

Larry was also a fat man and he was slightly taller than Willy, they had been friends since school so why had the bastard started fucking his wife. They were both forty-five and they were drinking buddies were no more.

Larry moved off behind some trees, "Got a lot of rabbit dropping here Willy?"

Willy took aim and lined up the sight with Larry's head, he didn't pause and pulled the trigger. Larry's head jerked forward and a line of blood flew into the air, the big man hit the ground dead. The next day Willy got back from the police station the police were not buying the accident story, they wanted to see him again this afternoon, but Willy had somewhere else to go to, he looked at the card.

He read the soul collector the woods stand in front of the line of trees and you will see. It was still day light when Willy stopped before the line of trees, he watched and then saw a white curtains between the trunks of the trees. He walked up to the curtain and pulled it back, he stepped inside and saw a vast jungle, he was immediately hot, and he was sweating like a fat pig. He could hear noises coming from the jungle noises that sounded as if they had never cried like that on earth. He saw a man at the edge of the woods, and walked over to him.

"Hello Willy."

"You look like the shop keeper."

"Yes, you met my brother, but I am a different creature altogether."

The man smiled and turned and walked into the jungle saying as he went.

"I am the soul collector."

Then as Willy watched a huge dragon came out of the jungle breathing fire, Willy screamed.

The police went round to Willy's place that night when he had failed to turn up at the station, his wife was out and the place looked like someone was in with all the lights turned on, so one of the police officers kicked the door in. They found Willy on the kitchen floor dead, a large hole in his forehead they could find no gun.

==

That evening the snow fell on the small village, a dark shadow appeared over the new shop, and there were noises coming from within the shadow, like the hammer hitting a nail into wood. The shadow disappeared and the shop keeper stood before the boarded-up shop.

"Time to move on," he said out loud and he changed into a devil like being, he had horns on his head and a wickedly long chin and he had hoofs for feet, he began to dance in the fresh snow. The next morning people starred in wonder as they saw the hoof marks in the snow. They went all down the streets sometimes over the cars and in people's gardens, they were all over the roofs of the houses. It was like some being had danced all over the village, and then people noticed that the shop was boarded up once more. (2013)

The end

FOURTEEN

Night time hell time

It was just another normal day in the town of Wainstone, the cars past the shops on the high street, the people walked down the pavements and the sun even shined through the clouds in the sky. Then that afternoon something strange happened. A hole opened up in the high street road at first it was a small hole, and then it collapsed inwards, and took up the whole of the road and pavement.

Luckily no one was driving at that moment, and no one was walking on the pavements of both sides. People stopped and stared, cars stopped before the hole and drivers got out to take a look at the hole. The police soon cordoned off the area and they put tape all round the scene, the hole disappeared into a dark void of nothing, police dropped rocks into the hole, but heard no sound, the hole was deep indeed.

Night time fell and the hole was the talk of the town, in pubs men chatted over their pints about the hole parents talked to their children about the hole over dinner. Rex Lane stood by the hole, trust his rotten luck to have to stand guard over the bloody hole all night, he had a hot date tonight, and now that was cancelled. He had tried to get someone else to do it, but no one wanted it and he had to do what his boss said he had no choice in the matter.

Rex was a large man standing well over six feet, he had a broken nose and looked like a boxer and a bald head to boot, but the fact was he had never stepped into the squared circle. He didn't mind fighting of course, but he was more of a lover than a fighter, and that date tonight damn she was so hot and ready for it too. He was twenty-three tomorrow and had hoped to get laid tonight what a birthday present that would have been; he sighed and kicked at a stone on the road.

He heard a sound from the hole, he turned to the hole and looked into the darkness, there was a swishing sound coming from the hole like something was coming up from a great distance. Then the sky was full of things, he couldn't see what they were it was way too dark, he felt something slimy attach to his face. He cried out as a hot pain ripped through his skin, another thing was climbing up his leg, and another wrapped around his back. He screamed as more and more creatures attacked him.

Roy was proud of his panic room he believed it was the only one in the whole town, but he loved his family dearly and money was no object to keeping them all safe. He admired the room; it was about six feet by six feet and had a television monitor that looked in the back garden, and the front of the house. There were tinned food and fruit on a shelf and books and a DVD player and television a selection of films to watch and bottled water.

He went into the living room and saw his wife Mandy sitting watching the soap operas she was still a fine-looking woman at forty. He was a year older than her, and she had long dark hair and looked Spanish, but was a hundred per cent English. The two kids Jason and Michelle were upstairs in bed he ran a hand through his thinning grey hair and sat down. He hated bloody soap operas, but what the hell there was a film on at ten o'clock a good one too 'Night of the vampires.'

He heard the noise first like a tapping on the window, he got up and went over to the large window in the living room, and he moved the red curtains and looked out. His mind didn't register what he saw at first, it looked like a small pig with sharp curled claws, it was tapping on the window, and it had a mouthful of wickedly sharp teeth, and one eye in its piggy face.

"What the fuck."

Mandy was by his side and put her hand to her mouth, now there was a lizard like thing crawling over the window, it had stump like feet and a razor-sharp tail which flicked back and forth. Then a larger shape appeared at the window.

"Move get the kids," he shouted at his wife.

She didn't need telling twice and raced for the stairs.

He closed the curtains hoping that the things would go away, he heard the window shatter slightly, but it held for now. He ran into the panic room and shortly after was joined by his family he closed the door as the living room window shattered inwards.

From the monitor he watched in horror at the things in the night, some of them buzzed as they flew in the air, he saw the flying ones had three eyes and eight stick like legs as they hovered by the camera. From the legs they shot out a web like substance he saw it hit the ground, and the ground began to bubble as the liquid turned it into mush. The large creature appeared at the camera it was hairy like a yeti, its mouth seemed to take up its whole face with sharp teeth inside, and it had one eye that was bright red, and it looked at the camera and with one swipe it took out the camera.

The monitor showed the back garden, things were crawling over the grass moving towards the house, they were green and worm like, sharp teeth like things coming from out of their blotted little bodies. Roy hoped that they would survive the night in the panic room, this was hell on earth and he would bet it was the hole which these creatures had come from.

Winston was drunk and he was enjoying it, his wife was out playing darts and he took advantage of that fact, and helped himself to the whisky from the bar. They both liked a drink and their bar was always well stocked tonight he had been bored on his own so he thought what the fuck lets drink. He wasn't really watching the television he was sipping his whisky and thinking to himself that he needed to pee badly. He heard the tapping at the window, he was so pissed.

"Fuck it," he shouted.

He remained in his chair, but he would have to move anyway he needed to pee. As he got to his feet the living room window shattered, he looked in shock as things crawled into his house. Little pig like things with curled claws and one single eye looking at him as they moved, things that buzzed in the air. Things he had never before seen in his life, one of the buzzing things squirted a liquid at him it caught him on the arm.

Pain shot through his arm and as he looked the liquid dissolved his flesh, his severed arm dropped to the floor and was at once taken by one of the pig like things. He screamed as he saw a large hairy monster climb through the window.

Nigel put his hand on his girlfriend's breast and rubbed it through her top, she moaned as they kissed under the bridge by the river, it was called 'Lovers Bridge' and many people from town had their first kiss under this bridge. Doris was well up for it tonight and that made Nigel very happy, they had yet to have sex, but he knew it was only a matter of time now. He was a lanky kid at eighteen and had short brown hair he was spotty, but good looking in a funny short of way, the girls seemed to like his looks anyway he was never short of a girlfriend.

Doris had been his girlfriend for three weeks now she was a kind girl with a good heart, she was on the plump side but she had a pretty face, and the largest tits Nigel had ever seen. She had shown him last week in her bedroom and they were huge and the nipples really poked out, you could hang your coat on them. His hand found her nipple now and he gently squeezed it, she moaned again and put her hand on his erection, God it felt like an iron bar.

Something smashed into his face and stuck there, it covered his mouth and he couldn't scream out, one of his eyes was covered as well and he saw Doris falling to the ground and slimy pulsing things crawled over her body. He felt intense pain as the thing on his face injected a hot liquid into his blood stream, another thing crawled up his leg and something went splash into the river. Nigel fell face first onto the dirt, and slimy things crawled over his body.

Day light came slowly for the town of Wainstone, the place was a mess, houses had their windows broken, thick slim lay on the roads and pavements, and the smell was like rotten eggs. Not many of the town's folks had survived the night and help came from outside, the army cleaned up the town and guarded the hole. Tony walked up to the hole he was in charge of this operation, he had to get that damned hole covered by night time and he had a plan.

"Hey Johnson get me the governor on the phone now."

"Sir Yes sir," a man saluted him and ran off.

He came back a few minutes later holding a hand-held phone he passed it to Tony.

"Yes, sir I have a plan and I need steel sheets and lots of them, very good sir thank you."

He looked at the hole they would cover it tonight and think what to do tomorrow maybe bombs thrown down the bloody thing. The steel sheets were delivered that day along with long steel poles, the poles were put across the hole on both sides and then the steel sheets laid on top, Tony hoped it would be enough. That evening Tony stayed with his men, they heard banging from the hole as things hit the steel, but after an hour or so the noise stopped.

"I think we have done it lads," Tony said to his men as he drank black coffee from a mug.

Tony yawned as he woke up and got up out of the cot, tents had been set up at night for him and his men and he walked out of the tent and looked at the steel sheets they had held.

"Jenkins's coffee."

Jenkins nodded at his boss, "Yes sir right away sir."

He stretched his back and ran a hand through his dark hair; the steel had held he was so pleased it was like a major victory against whatever those things had been.

"Your coffee sir."

He smiled at the short Jenkins with his crew cut and flat nose.

"Well Jenkins it looks like we sent them devils back to hell where they belong."

"Yes, sir and a good job too," Jenkins saluted and walked off.

He was about to return to his tent when he heard a shout from Dalton.

"Sir."

He watched as private Dalton ran up to him, he stopped and got his breath back before talking.

"It's bad sir really bad."

"What is man, tell me."

Tony was getting annoyed now.

"More hole's sir all over the country, and even in London loads of them sir opened up this morning."

Tony stared at the steel sheets the night mare had only just begun. (2013)

The end

C Robert Paul Bennett 2012/2013